I0684570

A BOOMER

IN INTENSIVE CARE

FROM THE ATOM BOMB TO THE END OF TIME

J.R. GOLD

Copyright

ISBN-13: 978-0-9994759-0-4

First Edition 2017

Dedication

It is the business, the burden of an enlightened
mind to tend, with compassion, to the
best which lies within each of us.
At times, it is necessary to develop a wrath
intended to right wrongs and to do away with
those few who would do away with us all.

About the Book

A Boomer in Intensive Care: From the Atom Bomb to the End of Time

An international conspiracy lead by American and Russian leaders and assisted by the Mafia is about to take control of world financial and military systems and establish a dictatorial New World Order.

The President of the United States, Rex Donald, in concert with his covert Russian ally, Anton Molinov, and aided by Capo de Capo Luigi Gentile, have formed a global cabal intended to subjugate humanity to their will and whim.

When former CIA operative Robert Santiago is hired by the President to assassinate Dr. Robert Marshall, his lifelong rival and the only man who has the means and vision to smash this insidious plot, Santiago faces a terrifying choice he never imagined.

Will the forces of evil seen throughout history strike a crushing blow to liberty and freedom? Will we be ruled by maniacal kleptocrats, or will the forces of truth break the ancient code in which history is doomed to repeat itself with suppression and domination by the few over the many?

This thrilling tale is informed by history and the appalling events of our time. In *A Boomer in Intensive Care: From the Atom Bomb to The End of Time*, a showdown unfolds that will keep you turning the pages.

Hold on for a wild ride into – and out of – darkness!

About the Author

With a double Ph.D. in biophysics and biomedical engineering, J.R. Gold has founded and directed several global technology companies. He has guided efforts to harness technologies developed at major corporations, defense labs, and universities. Dr. Gold has also been a principal of one of the world's foremost management and technology consulting firms.

Hailing from the Gold Coast of Long Island, New York, Dr. Gold holds several international patents and has lectured extensively around the world on innovation and creativity.

Having morphed into an investigative journalist, his previous non- fiction books, essays, and articles have been devoted to exposing corporate and political corruption. He has been an advisor to the U.S. Senate Finance Committee overseeing healthcare policy in the United States. Now turning to the freedom of fiction writing, Dr. Gold combines his keen sense of history with tales intended to engage, stimulate, and inform.

To

Anna, My Beloved: Till the End of Time

Contents

Preface

Another book? Another look? Why?

We are overwhelmed by constant streams of very disturbing and often specious information: news which informs us that the very foundations and assumptions concerning our society and the world are being shaken, possibly to death. Is this the end, the beginning of the end, the end of the end?

Each news report, every pundit, every pseudo press conference challenges our minds, senses, and even our reason. Often the spokespeople of the government of the United States are blatantly disingenuous and mean-spirited. They make no attempt to veil their hostility and bigotry. Are they the new Gestapo — our Gestapo?

Can this really be? Are the unfolding events just a continuation of the past or something terribly new and frightening? Is our current experience a new chapter in history or the past repeating itself?

Frozen in political gridlock, a stunned public looks on while rights are stripped, people grow sick, and protections of social protection fold. What are we being told? The sad answer is *lies*. Vacuous statistics touting an improved world while we stand at the brink of nuclear Armageddon, denied affordable medical care, paying higher taxes, and receiving decreasing social benefits. Do they think we're stupid?

Perhaps. Perhaps we are.

The story that unfolds in these pages of Dr. James Marshall and the assassin tasked by the sitting president of the United States with flicking him off the table is enriched by examples from history that suggest that these are, indeed, dangerous and unprecedented times.

The author has a definitive philosophical perspective: the struggle between light and dark forces is in play. The price for losing this ages-long battle is nothing less than the destruction of civilization.

Unbridled greed and the sharp teeth of the Mafia are now mixed with the highest levels of government. There is no illusion here: the dreams and fears of the actors in this play are real and terrifying.

Fascist Rex Donald, the sitting president of the United States, has directed an international cabal that transcends national interests. He is enacting a nuclear-tipped power grab in consort with other dark forces in Russia and Palermo, which treasonably betray the safety and well-being of the planet.

How far does this story of infamy stray from the nightly news?

Let the reader be the judge.

1

Setting the Stage

THE TRAJECTORY OF one's life is filled with a cacophony of inflection points, events, perceptions, and memories. For Dr. James Marshall, the recollection of his path is given greater dimension by the recall of smells, emotions, aspirations, and his biggest successes and most profound disappointments. The sweet cornucopia of sadness and tears of happiness and laughter.

The course of recollecting a single life can also be set in the context of history and the larger events swirling in the vortex of the world. As Dr. James Marshall continues in his journey, his own personal experiences have gained further momentum, in graphic detail and an appreciation that his time on the planet has not been lived in isolation.

Dr. Marshall has struggled, throughout his life, to understand the confrontation of good versus evil and anger versus compassion. He has realized the inherent difficultly most have in admitting the presence of evil in others: a kind of natural psychological protection mechanism which denies that dark forces exist and are often close at hand.

When faced with evil, what actions should be taken when these negative forces can impact the well-being and happiness of others?

How far should one go in nullifying those powers that menace an individual soul, let alone an entire populace?

We do not live in isolation: rather our lives, Dr. Marshall has discovered, are influenced by a confluence of energies in which a single person's destiny is intertwined with a much larger whole.

Carl Jung, the great German psychotherapist and philosopher, called such a fabric of events *zeitgeist*: the global unconscious mind, the spirit of the times, the connected minds of the planet's inhabitants.

Georg Wilhelm Friedrich Hegel, also a German psycho-spiritual seer, spoke about the unstoppable vectors of history. He called these vectors historic dialectics, the forces of nature that flow through all events like a freight train driven silently through each of our minds.

This spirit of zeitgeist runs through us all: expressed through us chickens running hither and yon, dancing to the tune of unheard music and affecting our individual and collective actions.

Dr. James Marshall has grown to understand that in his conscious and unconscious minds, his personal will, actions, and feelings are woven together with that of the collective mind.

This kind of awareness can occasionally be glimpsed through dreams. The dreams of Dr. James Marshall have been filled with moments of cerebral movies replete with sensuality and rendered in vivid detail. Some of these night visions are filled with delight. Many are hilarious and up-lifting, laughing while he sleeps.

Others are visions of entrapment without means of escape — dreams ending in awakened fear. A fear without hope of resolution.

While the stories of Dr. Marshall's nightmares vary, the premise does not.

For Dr. Marshall, the final news clips of the evening, watched before bed, may be churned into a story scripted by an unconscious mind not subject to the controls of rationality or the normal reason used to maneuver through a wakeful day. Sometimes this inner scriptwriter sleeps quietly. Other times, turbulent and prophetic cinematic epics spring into realistic detail, instilling a horrifying existential fright. These dream outcomes may provide either inspiration and instructive lessons or mortal dread. They also portend the sensation of helplessness and profound depression of having to continue to live in a tortured world.

In recanting the following living commentary, Dr. Marshall has now come face to face with his ultimate challenge — encountering a new manifestation of malevolence which threatens all life on the planet, a psychopath with his fingers poised over nuclear triggers.

On August 6, 1945, James Marshall was born in Alamogordo, New Mexico. It was the day Hiroshima was destroyed by a bomb like the one tested in his family's backyard on July 16 of that same year, not thirty days before. When little baby James saw the light of day for the first time, 200,000 people saw the same light as their last. Those who survived suffered unimaginable pain and sickness, for decades. Was this coincidence? An overture? A sign? A prelude of what was to come?

As James Marshall grew, all these questions became clearer and more precisely defined.

Does an ethical imperative operate which justifies taking extreme measures to stop yet another chapter of human genocidal history?

Aging now and able to appreciate the coming end of his days, Dr. Marshall has approached an appropriate time in life to reconcile his past and to take strong, compassionate action for an earthly future he is personally unlikely to experience.

Dr. Marshall has never been prone to violence, but extraordinary times require extraordinary measures. Concurrent with his philosophical conundrum, Dr. Marshall has learned that he is suffering from a life-ending disease: there is no diagnosis, but the final outcome is certain and, perhaps, soon.

He has pondered how to paint the canvas of his legacy. What colors to use, what perspectives to bring, what lessons to unfold, what actions to take: these are the complicated challenges of a complicated mind seeking to tell a complicated story, not just to others but to himself.

Dr. Marshall has learned to be careful about what he remembers and to be careful about who hears the story being told.

In physics, the Heisenberg uncertainty principle states that the position and the velocity of an object cannot both be measured exactly, at the same time, even in theory. The principle is not relevant in ordinary life, but at the sub-atomic level it becomes very important, where it means that observing a particle can change that which is being observed.

Like the tiny electron winging through the ether, when one embarks on an uncertain journey, it is likely that one will not end up where intended.

Dr. Marshall has come to think of himself as *A Boomer in Intensive Care*, a place where one goes knowing the forces of nature will ultimately prevail.

What should be done before the game is over, while he abides in a stopover of intensive care, waiting for the end of time?

2

Santa Fe, New Mexico

It is the business of the future to be dangerous
– Alfred North Whitehead

FAIR WARNING IS hereby given: I am a great pretender. The first time I met Dr. James Marshall, I thought he might be insane.

First impressions are not always accurate. I was to learn that I had accidentally met an extraordinary man dedicated to the pursuit of compassion in a world gone bad and mad.

In the waiting area of the emergency room at Santa Fe Hospital, the gentleman seated next to me was immaculately well-dressed in a double-breasted, raw silk blazer studded with gold buttons and a red and blue striped tie. He was well-tanned and handsome. His hair was shockingly silver and shining. He seemed relaxed and comfortable in his own skin.

I looked down, glancing at a magazine. When I raised my head and turned, Dr. James Marshall looked straight into my eyes; his glance pierced into me like a laser dart. Then he spoke with a soft but deliberate voice: no vocalized pauses, just an uninterrupted stream of consciousness.

He spoke to me as if he knew me. I came to realize that he knew me quite well, as if expecting our chance encounter.

What he began to expound belied a deep anxiety and dread. He seemed to be tortured and yet quietly reflective. A strange cocktail, indeed.

"Dr. James Marshall, here, and you?"

"It is a pleasure to meet you Dr. Marshall. I go by Robert Santiago. Please call me Santiago: my friends do and I would welcome the opportunity to count you among them."

"Santiago," he said, "those bastards have turned us into cannibals. Their cold-blooded agenda is ruthless and uncaring. The worst of the worst have risen to the pinnacles of power. The cartel of the heartless has seized the power they have always sought. They are craven and will settle only for the totalitarian control they have always sought.

"To think," he continued, "that I grew up with these monsters! They were my *neighbors*, for God's sake. I played with them as a child and knew their parents. I watched as these post-World War II New York Jewish businessmen, mostly hiding behind gentile pseudonyms, slowly grew comfortable with extending their power by amassing massive wealth, often gained at the expense of others!

"Yes, I did grow up in the lap of luxury and was bathed in a supercilious kind of greed that fundamentally disregarded and disrespected others. Yet, as a kid, I admired the oligarchs-in-waiting and their bravado — their buildings and industries. Some, like Rex Donald, built cities of slums on either side of the Long Island Expressway in New York, towers of despair too numerous to count. Too gloomy to stomach.

"Yes, I realized later that people like Mr. Donald were the progenitors of constructing cities designed to warehouse the lower classes, the struggling and underprivileged.

"I knew even as a boy that there was something evil about such enterprises, yet I admired him and the cluster of other emerging tycoons who populated the enclaves of my childhood.

"I did not know then, that many, including Mr. Arnold Donald and my own father, had close ties with the Brooklyn, Staten Island, and Jersey *Mafiosi*. I did not know then that nothing would stop them in their pursuit of power and money. Nothing. Nothing!

"The mobster Italians of New York were actually Jews disguised as practicing Catholics. The Jews, like the Italians, disguised themselves with gentile names like Marshall, Johnson, or Donald, pretending to practice religion because they thought a mandatory bar mitzvah was good for the kids: it was a sham, a show. But a five-hundred-thousand-dollar bar mitzvah was an ideal time to broadcast a message that the golden threshold had been crossed.

"These ostentatious parties followed the hysterics of a stressed adolescent reading from the Torah. These soirées were really designed to bring together the "club," away from the prying eyes of the FBI.

"The Jews and Italians of New York were interwoven. The Italians needed the Jews for their brains, while the Jews needed the Italians for their brawn and unabashed ability to permanently silence anyone who stood in the way of progress.

"Both cultures thrived on copious amounts of great food and drink, trophy women, and the obligatory Cuban cigar. They loved to yell, back slap, hug, and gesticulate. These two ethnic cultures were made for each other. A match made in heaven, so to speak!"

This was a kind of rap, a rant really. To approach an apparent stranger, in the wink of an eye, with such a telling discourse. This was not something I had ever experienced. But then Dr. Marshall hardly seemed to be an ordinary man.

I thought Dr. Marshall might be on the brink of plunging into a mental abyss. Yet his *tone* contained *facts,* facts that painted a picture of a world all too familiar to me. His speech was much too detailed to be a product of a mind gone wild. It was too consistent with what I knew to be true: he was talking about the underbelly of humanity. These were the dim streets which I have walked for most of my life.

What was Dr. Marshall doing here? He didn't look like he required medical attention, but first impressions can be misleading. Why was he lost in despondency — a kind of gloomy miasma, a pall of melancholy and self-reproach? What was this agony about?

I was afraid to interrupt the progression of his thought, yet I had become engrossed. I wanted to know more.

His full-throated monologue continued:

"At that time, I did not realize that my own father was an active player in a pitiless and unapologetic world of men and children who were destined to become oligarchs and even... presidents.

"My father, Santiago, used to refer to our next-door neighbor's son as Little Boy, after the atomic bomb dropped on Hiroshima. I suppose my father thought of this vicious little mongrel, Rex Donald, as being like one of his New Mexico nuclear kids.

"Frankly, in my eyes, Rex was more like Fat Man, but as a kid, he was neither rotund nor a man! That would change decades later when my next-door neighbor took the oath of office on the Capitol steps. Who would have thought? What can I tell you? That little shit was born under a bad sign."

President! Did Dr. Marshall know me? How could he? Did he?

The nurse came out into the waiting room. "Dr. Marshall," she said, "perhaps you'd be more comfortable in our private anteroom. It's next to our intensive care unit and reserved for those who require privacy." He stood up and smiled warmly at each of us as he glanced around the room.

It had become clear to me that he had been completely aware of his surroundings. Nothing mad here. But why had he spoken, openly, about my client, the sitting president of the United States?

Before he left my side, he bent down and whispered close to my ear.

"I suppose I'm not an ordinary bystander, Santiago. I have accomplished a lot in my years, and am a student of history who, among other areas of interest, has closely studied the unimaginable events that took place in the high desert of New Mexico. Atomic events that changed the world forever. I have always closely followed the unfolding of world events and the key players who have been, and are, the current principal actors on the global stage.

"The suffering of so many fills and chills the air. There are ghosts roaming in our thoughts reminding us that evil cannot, should not, kill the better instincts of the miraculous confluence of cosmic events which gave us all this precious *life*.

"The blood suckers who now hold power in this country are deadly and dangerous players.

"The Mafia has risen to power with nuclear weapons: a mafia running a sovereign state with nuclear weapons!

"Would you agree with me, Santiago, that they need to be stopped?"

Without waiting for an answer, Dr. Marshall followed the nurse through a door near the front desk of the emergency room.

Dr. Marshall, I knew, was a renowned physicist and former United States ambassador to Russia. He had retired to his estate here in the Santa Fe Mountains.

His father, Dr. Norman Marshall, had been one of the key brains behind the Manhattan Project and a close friend of Dr. Robert Oppenheimer, the progenitor of the atomic bomb at Los Alamos, not thirty-five miles distant from downtown Santa Fe.

Dr. Norman Marshall had been at the Trinity Test site when the first atomic bomb, nicknamed "The Gadget," was tested atop a tower in the desert near Alamogordo, New Mexico in the summer of 1945. Shortly thereafter, two bombs built at Los Alamos, Little Boy and Fat Man, were dropped on Japan, ending one of the bloodiest conflicts in history.

Dr. Norman Marshall became extraordinarily wealthy by buying up uranium mines throughout the world, principally in Kazakhstan, Canada, and Australia. I suppose he correctly anticipated the dangerous cosmic game that was about to unfold.

He also understood that a treasure could be realized from the unleashed fury hidden in atoms and this treasure could and would likely fall into the undeserving hands of petty, greedy and evil men — men willing to pay any price for power.

I had heard that after the war, Dr. Norman Marshall moved back to his home town of New York to raise his family and manage what was to become one of the world's great fortunes, built by supplying, on a nearly exclusive basis, the raw materials with which the United States and other countries would build the deadliest arsenals in the history of mankind.

James Marshall, his son, emerged as a mighty and potent force himself. With an outstanding intellect and multiple degrees from MIT and Caltech, he was a founder of a company called Intela, creating yet another technology that revolutionized the way we live: the microprocessor.

I had known about this man and his accomplishments in business, science, and government. I had *no* idea, though, about the extent of his agitation. I had no idea why. But in the few minutes of that first meeting in the Santa Fe Hospital ER, I felt a strange empathy, an emotion quite foreign to me.

I had a twinge of regret that my real mission was to prepare for his elimination.

I approached the nursing station and the attendant who had escorted Dr. Marshall to his private quarters. I lied, with no hesitation, that I had accompanied Dr. Marshall to the hospital and would appreciate the opportunity to sit with him. I politely told her to ask him if the fellow sitting next to him in the public waiting room could join him. After disappearing for a few moments, she re-entered and motioned me to follow her to a small room where Dr. James Marshall sat quietly, staring into space.

I sensed the weight resting on his shoulders. I had known the great and powerful and knew they were mortal, vulnerable, and immune from neither the toll of time nor the complexity and machinations of the human mind.

At the end of the day, we all stare into the space beyond this life: rich or poor, powerful or not. I sensed that Dr. Marshall had seen this as well. I was about to learn why and how.

"I felt your presence out there," he said. "We look to be about the same vintage. I would welcome your companionship, Santiago. It might do us both good."

An unexpected window to the rest of my life was about to unfold. The moment he invited me into his world, I had no idea that the man I was sent to kill would change my life.

I also did not know that Dr. James Marshall knew who I was and was expecting me!

3

Alamogordo, New Mexico

Behind every great fortune lies a great crime.
— Balzac

"SO, YOU REALLY want to know what brought me to this place?" said Dr. Marshall in a quiet voice. "Are you sure you want to know? Do you want the twenty-thousand-foot view or do you want to go granular?"

"Granular, Dr. Marshall," I replied. "I want to hear it all. But before we begin, I am quite concerned about you and your despondency. I know who you are but had no inkling of your suffering. What happened?"

"This is going to take some time," he replied. "But if you're willing to listen, I'm willing to tell."

I agreed.

"Life is an experience of many colors and flavors," he began, "of thoughts and aspirations, of intended and accidental events, of mistakes and regrets, of joy and jokes, of music and delight and rivers of tears.

"The Buddhists say that the answer to *samsara* does not lie in *samsara*. It lies in a higher, parallel and transcendental universe. It is only there that one can be happy and free, perhaps forever.

"In other words, don't look for answers in the day-to-day rulebook: truth lies elsewhere. This was the great wisdom of a great mind: Buddha Shakyamuni. I'll get to telling you more about that.

"You should understand what I mean when I say *samsara*: it's the endlessly repeated cycles of birth, misery, and death caused by karma. Once you get it right, you win the door prize to infinite freedom. Bad karma reaps the unfortunate reward of having to go back and start all over again: for most, forever.

"You'd think only a fool would repeat the mistakes that condemn one to a succession of unhappy lifetimes. But we live in a world of fools, myself, at times, included.

"Have you ever felt completely happy? Free? Safe? Joyful? Satisfied? Complete?

"In one way or the other, I've been looking for the door to this kind of freedom all of my life. But let me try and tell you about that in some kind of sequence. The road has been torturous and, in reflection, I have tried to make some sense of how all the events, good and bad, have added up to the conclusion of being, here, now.

"Where to begin?"

Dr. Marshall went silent for quite a long time, gazing out, seemingly focused on nothing and everything. A movie of his life shown to him alone, I guessed, played at the speed of light and mind.

"OK," he said, "let's start where I started: Alamogordo, New Mexico. My father brought home two puppies, big little guys with giant paws and active wet red tongues. One was black, the other tan. I loved those guys from the start. They still fill my heart.

"My father was a big man. He said one of the dogs was called Fat Man and the other Little Boy! He also plucked from his pocket a little white cat: he said its name was Pluto, short for plutonium. I thought that was funny. Kids are suckers for funny words.

"I was to later understand that it was funny, but not for reasons that a child could comprehend. My father did not tell me that I had other brothers whom he had fathered: Fat Man and Little Boy and they were not dogs! It would take me some years to fill in the gaps.

"I learned something about the world of mystical thought from my father's close friend and colleague, Dr. J. Robert Oppenheimer. He was a frequent visitor to our house in Alamogordo. My father told me to call him Dr. O, or Opie.

"Oppenheimer was phenomenal: he was a brilliant theoretical physicist, astrophysicist, astronomer, mathematician — this list of his interests would take me an hour to recite.

"Unlike many scientific geniuses focused solely on science, Oppenheimer was deeply interested in the arts, religion, literature, music and mysticism. He was curious about just about everything, including Communism.

"During the McCarthy witch hunt, the latter interest got him into deep water.

"Parenthetically, Oppenheimer grew up with works by Picasso, Monet, and Lautrec hanging on the walls of his family home in New York City. He had been exposed to art and culture from the get-go. He was unquestionably a great genius. It has been said by people who knew him well that Dr. O was particularly interested in Hindu thought. He had a feeling of mystery about the universe that surrounded him, like a fog.

"His longtime lover, an avowed communist and practicing psychiatrist named Jean Tatlock, who tragically committed suicide just before the Trinity test, exposed Oppenheimer to the writings of John Donne. Opie latched onto a passage, one of many, from Donne: *'If the radiance of a thousand suns were to burst at once into the sky, that would be like the splendor of the mighty one.'* How profound for the person directly responsible for enabling the technology which would forever alter the course of this world.

"With Donne front of mind, he knew that unleashing the power of the universe is not just an act of man, but of God. This was Oppenheimer's business from 1943 to the summer of 1945.

"We all know that after succeeding with this stupendous effort he became deeply depressed when he realized his responsibly for the deaths and maiming of several hundred thousand people fewer than thirty days after the Gadget exploded on the Trinity tower in New Mexico.

"He visited President Truman, begging Truman to bar the future use of atomic weapons, and pleading that he, Robert Oppenheimer, had the blood of thousands on his hands, as he recited the Bhagavad Gita: *Now I am become death, the destroyer of the world!*

"Einstein and many other scientists also pleaded with the government to discontinue the use of atomic weapons: most all were judged subversive. Many were permanently disenfranchised.

"Truman threw Oppenheimer out of the Oval Office and told his staff, 'I don't want to see that son of a bitch in this office ever again.'

"In 1946, a year later, President Truman, himself struck with regret, awarded Oppenheimer the Metal of Merit. Yet, despite this presidential recognition, Oppenheimer was forever stripped of his security clearance, ostracized and humiliated by the McCarthy-era inquisition: his serious involvement with Communism was too much for Edgar Hoover and the other big boys to stomach.

"This dichotomy has never been lost on me. Society punished the man who created the instrument that ended a global conflagration and then turned to regret what he had worked so diligently to create. His entire being had been focused on the creation of a device that physically realized Einstein's theoretical calculations. He was the parent to a terrible mechanism that brought a peaceful end to war. The means to achieve massive destruction ran counter to Oppenheimer's exposure to the humanism implicit in Hindu and Buddhist thought — ideas that were deeply embedded in his consciousness.

"Once the cat was out of the nuclear bag, it could never be put back in. Oppenheimer knew this. In other words, Oppenheimer was mired in overwhelming regret."

Dr. Marshall paused. I could see his eyes tear. He scrubbed his face with his hand as if to wash away a haunting dream.

"The instructive lesson I took from my encounters with Oppenheimer," he continued, "is that our personal journeys in life are happening in the context of history. In the case of Dr. O, he was not merely influenced by an external event separate and distinct from himself: he had *precipitated* that event! He was not just influenced by history: he *created it.*

"As soon as I was old enough to really make sense of these kinds of things, this realization influenced the way I have come to view my own life. Is my journey a path I have traveled alone, influenced by events: or am I a creator of history? What threads of the fabric of history have been woven into me, made me, or have been made by me? I felt that Oppenheimer was a kindred traveler: a scientist and philosopher. I have always admired that in him and have sought, where possible, to realize his better qualities in myself.

"I think that's a fair question for all of us to ask about the meaning of our lives.

Momentous events have transpired in the century in which we have both lived, Santiago. How have they shaped you? Those who you know? Those who you don't?"

"Dr. Marshall," I replied, "my story is a long one. Let's just say that I am feeling a real comradeship with you. I have struggled to understand where I began and where I may end. I think about black holes, and whether I am in or out of one! I'm joking, but not completely!"

I realized that Dr. Marshall had been speaking to me in fluent Castilian Spanish. My Latin accent was probably unmistakable. I complimented him on his perfect inflection. Spanish, the kind spoken in Madrid, requires a good ear and an expert tongue!

He told me that Oppenheimer's fascination with languages, including Sanskrit, had inspired Oppenheimer to learn Spanish, Mandarin, Russian, French, German, Italian, Hindi, Hebrew, Arabic, and Japanese. Dr. Marshall said Oppenheimer was fluent in all.

I told Dr. Marshall that, although I had been born in Madrid, I had always considered myself to be a citizen of the world. I omitted that I had spent the better half of my life as an operative for the CIA.

I also did not tell him the reason I was drawing him in. But, Dr. Marshall was no fool.

"OK, Santiago," he said, "I'm glad we met. Hopefully, I can get to know you as well, *compadre!* At my age, there are not too many people left with whom I can share this kind of repartee. Before launching into more of this, I want you, Santiago, to know that ethics and compassion are important to me — very important. Especially, I think, because I grew up in a world in which I saw terrible greed and avarice. I have been witness to the worst that human beings can be. Sometimes, the best.

"For me, the tensions between right and wrong, good and evil are not abstractions.

"Listen, where Oppenheimer was a model for me — not a perfect one, by any means — my father was not.

"Unfortunately, although brilliant, he walked on the dark side. I never considered him to be a model for my life, but acorns do not fall far from the tree. Where I considered Oppenheimer to be noble, my father was not. I always knew that.

"You asked about my despondency. It began the day that my childhood nemesis, Rex Donald, took the oath of office as president of the United States.

"The little bastard I knew as a kid now has the power to annihilate the planet: the very power that Oppenheimer and my own father helped to build. He is not even close to being worthy of such responsibility.

"He is the child of a heartless, callous slum lord. Arnold Donald. 'Fat Man,' as I called his son, was taught by experts to use people, to lie when convenient, and to kill when necessary. Like Rex, I come from a privileged world in which my own father became quite rich. Arnold Donald was a friend of my father and our neighbor on the Gold Coast of Long Island.

"Both Norman, my father, and Arnold Donald grew powerful through their ruthless grab for money, influence, and unbridled power. They both walked on what I call the dark side.

"These people were examples, models to which I was exposed as a young man. I am no angel and have had my own devils and mistakes with which I contend. Some were terrible mistakes. But I came out, I think, with hope and respect for those who are suffering and abandoned.

"However, the monsters of my youth are now the monsters of my old age!

"Despondency doesn't even come close to describing my sadness: my wrath: I am afraid for us all.

"This is no ordinary melancholia. This is fear and trembling. This is a Dali painting of a barren existential landscape spread out before my feet and...yours.

"Listen, Santiago, I forgot to tell you that we left Alamogordo in 1946 as my father and Dr. O were winding down their involvement with The Manhattan Project. My father felt that living that close to Trinity might be dangerous. The Geiger counter readings were off the charts and the wind had been blowing towards Alamogordo on the days after the Gadget exploded.

"My father mistakenly thought that a move to Truth or Consequences, New Mexico, would be a safe enough distance away: one hundred and thirty-seven miles. He was dead wrong.

"Although we only stayed in Truth or Consequences for a short time before moving to New York, the silent threat of serious illness still hovers over what is left of our family and over me.

"What a prophetic name: Truth or Consequences. I have lived to experience both the truth and the consequences. Foretelling, don't you think Santiago?"

In a pattern of behavior to which I was becoming accustomed, Dr. Marshall did not wait for an answer, but kept his thoughts flowing unabated.

"The biological effects of radiation fallout were not well understood in those days, but there was enough data to suggest that it could be serious. As it turned out, the fallout from that test resulted in terrible illnesses for residents of the surrounding test site area and the supervisory military personnel.

"There's more. The testing at Trinity was actually halted while the scientific community debated whether a nuclear explosion would actually cause a chain reaction, igniting the entire atmosphere, enveloping the globe. There was real concern, enough so that the issue was brought before secret Congressional bodies and President Truman. This is not bullshit, *amigo*.

"It was decided that the risk was worth taking. The lives of the surrounding population were of little concern. The lives of the military personnel were irrelevant.

"I suppose the scientists and engineers thought that they were immune from any consequence. My father was not as skeptical as he should have been. Our little family was along for the ride: he was the driver.

"Since 1945, Hispanic families living near the Trinity site have struggled with cancer and radiation-related illnesses. Seventy years later, the radiation level in southern New Mexico is ten thousand times higher than the Centers for Disease Control defines as being safe for public areas. Santa Fe County, home to Los Alamos, has cancer rates far exceeding national averages — seven decades *ex post facto!*

"July, when the Gadget blew, is the rainy season in New Mexico. For a month after the explosion, fallout literally rained down on the farms and homes of the residents, contaminating food, clothing, the air, water — everything.

"Senators from New Mexico are now suing the federal government on behalf of the citizens of the state. The government provided *no* warnings to local residents to evacuate. Most of those families who have died off were poor, ethnic minorities. They were like guinea pigs.

"The vulnerable were dispensable then, and they remain expendable now. My old archenemy, President Rex Donald, has openly stated that he doesn't really see why we don't use our nuclear weapons more often! He was an idiot as a boy: he is even more of a schmuck now.

"I remember, as adolescents, our discussions about the atomic bomb. Back then, he thought it was a great idea. He also thought the Holocaust was probably a fake, a made-up lie: propaganda. Strange for a Jewish kid who should have known better, but sick people live in their own bizarre worlds.

"Santiago, I tape recorded the conversations I had with the Fat Man, our President. I was incredulous then. Now I am horrified because I know what's always been on his mind. God help us, he now has his finger on the button. He now has the launch codes.

"We're not talking about a normal person. In my eyes it's incredible that this boy, Fat Man, now is a nod away from causing global Armageddon.

"Santiago, I still have those tapes. Rex Jr. built a fortune on the backs of others without a care. He may not remember, but I do.

"He is ruthless. A sociopath and pathological narcissist. Do you know the song by The Talking Heads, 'Psycho Killer, *Qu'est-ce que c'est?*' Have a listen sometime!

"You ask me why I am despondent?

"Santiago, do you know the difference between anger and wrath? If you don't, I'm going to provide you with a lesson taught to me by a Buddhist master. We'll get to that in a bit.

"In the name of mankind, Rex Donald must be stopped. I have agonized over how I might accomplish what must be done.

"Let's take a break. I think I need some fresh air. Perhaps a drink or two? What do you say?"

4

Treachery

*I have learned to hate all traitors, and there is
no disease that I spit on more than treachery*

– Aeschylus

I WAS GROWING TO like Dr. Marshall. This man exuded power and poise. You don't often find people of high moral purpose.

My affection for Dr. Marshall was soon to be proven unfortunate.

As we entered an elegant Santa Fe cantina, I excused myself for a brief stop in the restroom. My phone alerted me to an awaiting message: "$5,00,000 wired to your Cayman account. You get more when I know more!"

5

Fade to Black

*Neither a wise man nor a brave man lies
down on the tracks of history to wait for
the train of the future to run over him.*

– Dwight D. Eisenhower

Dr. Marshall was seated at the end of the bar. His lips pressed together in a slight grimace. He was pensive. Conflicted.

"Ah, Santiago, please have a seat. What would you like to drink? Join me, perhaps in a shot of some Anejo tequila — I know some really good stuff!"

After a shot, he seemed buoyed. He ordered another and proceeded on with his reflection.

"You know, history is filled with inflection points. Vortices where massive events collide and profound change results. Usually there is a single being at the epicenter of such world-changing events. For whatever reason, these points of influence radiate like the ripples of a stone thrown into the center of a still pond. They provide us with lessons.

"These lessons must not be forgotten. They should not be wasted.

"When we spot weeds growing in our garden, history informs us that, unless they are stopped, choked, and destroyed, they will engulf the golden fruit of humankind and leave a desolate and hopeless world wondering why the sun disappeared.

"Usually, there are significant individuals who are at the root of historic, dialectic, and often diabolic changes.

"Some of these history-moving individuals are demons from hell, from the dark side.

Others are uplifting geniuses whose effects enliven us all. Like Mozart or Buddha.

"Interesting how the truly evil ones can be recalled unhesitatingly. The humanists and artists — those who have positively changed the course of history — sit more quietly in the background.

"The maniacs jump out up front. Their effects are usually enormous and cataclysmic.

It is this struggle between good and evil, between probity and iniquity, which has long captured my mind's eye. I frame my views of nearly all that I see with this ever-present polarity.

"I can think of a few pieces of evil, like the assassination of Archduke Ferdinand in 1914, deliberately staged by the Germans, who were gaming for an excuse to take over Europe and Russia. The loss of life in the First World War was forty million. The destruction was profound, the devastation and starvation unthinkable.

"This terrible inferno was primarily the handiwork of Kaiser Wilhelm, a narcissistic egomaniac spoiling for conquest. The radius of his influence and the human beings who suffered was immense. One man with the power to create Hades on earth. One man.

"The Second World War resulted in the deaths of over eighty million people. How could this have happened? Its roots went back to November 11, 1918. The Germans were destroyed and the war reparations exacted from Germany for their demonic onslaught so antagonized the Motherland that they give birth again, less than twenty years later, to yet another monstrous war and one of the greatest monsters in all history.

"This catastrophe was the handiwork of Adolph Hitler, another mega-sociopath and narcissistic egomaniac also spoiling for conquest. The radius of his influence was immense, and millions fell victim to his hypnotic powers, making ordinary people into ruthless killing machines.

"Over one hundred and twenty million people died within a thirty-year span. This does not include the war in the Pacific: thirty-six million more dead!

"One man with the power to create incalculable destruction and death. Let's not forget that, in the process, Hitler and his cronies accomplished the largest ethnic cleansing of entire populations in all history. One man.

"A single bullet could have put an end to this horrifying chapter in human history. A few aborted attempts to wipe him away were made, but all failed until Hitler himself fired a shot to his own head. But it was too late. Too late!

"In a span of only thirty years, over one hundred and fifty million people were murdered, starved, or maimed. These kinds of statistics disorient the imagination. Human beings possess a unique inability to see evil in others. I think this is an automatic mechanism to shield the soul.

"Europe was destroyed and needed to be rebuilt. The entire planet was affected by this insanity. Ironic that Germany is, again, one of the most powerful countries in the world. An economic juggernaut, they assert power with industry and money. It's a modern form of warfare.

"Another prelude to today's world order came in 1917, with a little affair called the Russian Revolution. This ideological earthquake set the stage for the birth of the Soviet Union, one of the most powerful philosophical states of the twentieth century. Was this the achievement of one man, Vladimir Lenin? Was the isolation of the czars an invitation to a complete reshuffling of the Russian social deck?

"Interesting that the aristocratic dominance of the Romanoff's was replaced by the choke hold control exerted by the elite Communist leaders, who installed themselves as a new elite of strongman leaders, dictators, and now, oligarchs.

"Comrade Stalin, for example, killed an estimated forty million of his own countrymen. This does not include the soldiers slaughtered in battle, pushing back the invading Germans.

"Another wormhole: The Wall Street Crash of 1929, which submerged the world into The Great Depression, putting millions around the world out of work for more than a decade. This was the product of the copulation of the Jazz Age with an untethered Wall Street given to unbridled greed. It was the dance of the lascivious Charleston, which ended in a deeply degraded worldwide social, political and economic catastrophe.

"I don't believe any one man can be held responsible for this particular cataclysm. Rather it was the collective greed of a population enjoying freedom from the First World War and the spoils reaped by the immeasurable gluttony of an entire system: banks, brokers, and a population content to let the 'good times roll — *laissez les bons temps roulez*.' This was without restriction or regulation.

"Greasing the skids: a government asleep at the wheel.

"You might think of this as the work of the collective mind, acting in harmony, in essence creating a single-minded being with an insatiable appetite. This is what Hegel and Jung referred to as *zeitgeist*: the collective mind. Unbounded greed is a zero-sum game. It could not stand."

Dr. Marshall cleared his throat, took another shot of Anejo and continued to share his thinking.

"Certainly the atomic bombings of 1945 should be considered as one of the pivotal events of history. Oppenheimer was not evil, but he did orchestrate the massive effort that is top of mind to us, even to this day.

"The Second World War was over, and what followed was a burst of prosperity in America. This was while Europe was being reconstructed from total ruin. But once the world of the powerful get a taste for war, it's hard to go on a peaceful diet. So, we again entered into new conflicts — Korea, Vietnam, Afghanistan, Iraq.

"Killing is good for business. That gluttony has not stopped.

"I think you can catch my drift here, Santiago. I don't have to beat this concept to death. The human species has left a trail of both great and awful things. Aleksandr Solzhenitsyn was succinct: 'The battle line between good and evil runs through the heart of every man.'

"In 1963, President John F. Kennedy was assassinated. The official explanation is one I know to be false. The

Warren Commission was a puppet show. Pretty impressive to get a Supreme Court chief justice to knowingly participate in one of history's most perverted cover-ups! Who would think that a Supreme Court justice could be bought? The ugly truth is that nearly anyone can be had: it's a matter of striking the right bargain with the devil.

"Lee Harvey Oswald was hardly a lone gunman. Jack Ruby was no accident. My father and his fellow oligarchs saw to that. Arnold Donald, my neighbor as a kid, was head of that little steering committee. I'll tell you more about that later.

"So who were the evildoers behind this staggering episode in history?"

I was astounded by what Dr. Marshall had just told me: that his father and the father of my current client had a hand in the killing of a president and the orchestration of the cascading events which followed that dreadful day in Dallas.

This was not just another assignment for a hired gun. I was now sitting on the edge of posterity and about to jump into it — into *making* it. This was the deep end of the pool. The water there is black. There is no bottom.

Dr. Marshall looked me squarely in the eye. He knew that he had just opened a box that could never be closed.

This man had a ringside seat to history. Now, in one way or another, we were both about to step into that arena together, making or breaking destiny. I knew it, but not for the reasons I contemplated at that bar in Santa Fe.

I had begun to understand why the president had sent me to dispatch Dr. Marshall.

He had known Dr. Marshall for his entire life and remembered well their association over the years, beginning in childhood and, intermittently, through the decades in which their paths diverged and crossed. He knew Dr. Marshall was intensely moral — and therefore dangerous. Dr. Marshall might step out of the shadows and put him down, like a sick dog. It was no secret that the president of the United States was a sham. He had pushed his way to the highest office in the world through chicanery and manipulation. Now that he had assumed office, he could no longer hide behind his vacuous rhetoric or the empty promises made to a public desperate for salvation — a public that Rex Donald despised, but needed in order to get what he wanted.

His need to be loved and admired was pathological. His narcissism was a psycho-dramatic attempt to make up for the fundamental insecurities of his childhood. As a human being, he was a loser and a user.

As a president: he was becoming a global menace. The public had been slow to catch on to his tricks and double talk. But slowly, the gravity of his ignorance could no longer be hidden. His mindless rants could no longer be ignored.

Yes, my business is assassination. It started with my years at the CIA in which *carte blanche* was given to me to rearrange entire countries, to quietly murder those who threatened the interests not only of the government, but the industrial and economic behemoths to whom Washington was beholding. We dispatched our missions without any moral turpitude. Standing over a body whose brains had just been blown out was, for me, business as usual.

Killing children and women, when required, were equally unimpressive, but perhaps I have, to preserve my sanity, shut such events out of my conscious mind.

After my time with the CIA, I had come to a place where I experienced a kind of epiphany: that perhaps my decades of blind brutality might have been wrong. I never dwelled on this, but the cold blood which had flowed in me had gradually warmed: but was not yet hot.

I was still a killer, hired now to do another unthinkable killing. I was paid well and had prospered working for foreign and domestic actors alike. Central and South America were familiar hunting grounds for me.

Assisting in overthrowing governments by eliminating those at the top was a game with which I was all too familiar.

Dr. Marshall motioned to the bartender, who then pointed to the front door. I turned to see several large men wearing black leather jackets enter and quickly circulate around the bar. I did not stand up because I knew there was no escape: I had walked into the trap. The men quietly escorted patrons away, telling them with smiles that their tabs had been paid. Then the front door was locked and the window shades looking out on the street front pulled closed.

The men surrounded me. Their concealed guns were quickly drawn.

Dr. Marshall spoke softly but deliberately. "Santiago, slowly put your weapon on the bar. We will continue our discussion in a more suitable place. You see, Santiago, I know who you are. I know why you're here. I know who sent you."

I placed my silver plated 1911 Colt 45 on the bar.

Suddenly, I felt a sharp jab in my neck. Fade to black.

6

Moral Aspirations

I REGAINED CONSCIOUSNESS. WHILE the drug with which I had been injected had rendered me totally unconscious, once I had reawakened its effects wore off rapidly.

I was seated next to Dr. Marshall in a very large circular room fitted with wraparound fourteen-foot floor-to-ceiling windows. The views were expansive and unobstructed: endless high desert rimmed by mountains. Santa Fe town is about 7,500 feet above sea level. The house appeared to be a good two thousand feet higher, nestled into a magnificent rocky peak. Santa Fe could be seen in the distance, to the south.

"I have known your employer for most of my life," Dr. Marshall said. "We have been expecting you. Rex Donald's senior aide works for me. His name is George Slater. You are acquainted with him, I believe.

"I know about the five million dollars deposited in your Cayman account. I know about your history with the CIA. I know you are a hired assassin. Perhaps when we're done you'll have a different view about who really needs to be 'removed.'

"I know more about you, Santiago, than *you* know about you!

"Rex Donald, our illustrious president, is a pretty bad actor. Perhaps one of the worst ever. To think that he rose to such power boggles my mind; but, as they say, shit happens!"

Dr. Marshall was quite casual in his speech, almost whimsical.

"Let me be clear, Santiago: Rex has set out to destroy this country. For decades he and Russian President Milonov have been planning to assemble a new world order. Neither has any allegiance to their countries. Their only loyalties are to themselves, their families, and to a lesser extent, their inner circles and their military forces.

"They have systematically undermined every social institution and have neutered their populations by overt and covert means of suppression. They have burrowed deeply into every aspect of their respective societies, including energy, communications, economics and health.

"They believe they are endowed by some divine right and are entitled to absolute authority and control over all living things. Their governments are a ruse for oligarchy: a small group exercising control especially for corrupt and selfish purposes. They have enforced their dominance with overwhelming military force and nuclear weapons.

"The earth is not sufficient territory for either: they now also seek to control space!

"Information has been comprehensively collected about nearly every human being on the planet. This information, like that gathered by the Nazis, informs their ability to conduct mass mind control and, if necessary, total subjugation and elimination.

"In short, Santiago, the man who sent you to take me out is, in his words, 'a beauty!'"

I was a captive now. It was clear to me that I would leave Dr. Marshall's enclave neither alive nor willingly.

"We spoke before about the difference between wrath and anger." Dr. Marshall was proceeding to address me in a friendly tone — strange for someone who was confronting a man sent to silence him forever.

"You see, Santiago, Rex Donald and his Russian counterpart, Anton Milonov, are about ready to make their biggest move. For the last decade, my associates around the world and I have been tracking both. We know everything and have firsthand knowledge, spies I think you would call them, planted in every country on the planet.

"Rex Donald's ascension to the presidency of the United States, coupled with Russia's Milonov being in control, represents the culmination of years of planning and scheming. They have infiltrated every institution: every branch of the military is poised to do their bidding.

"What they do not know is that for every action there is an equal or opposite reaction. My associates and I around the world have installed concurrent counteracting forces in every institution that Rex Donald and Anton Milonov have infiltrated.

"We are not going to allow the human species to become subjugated to their capricious whims or tyranny.

"So, back to the wrath-versus-anger question. As I may have intimated, my early exposure to J. Robert Oppenheimer had a profound effect on me. He was fascinated by the Hindu mystics, close cousins to Buddhism, on whose teachings I have calibrated my spiritual compass.

"I have also spent years training in the art of Shaolin Kung Fu.

"I have studied under great masters of Buddhist thought. Conflated with my martial arts training, I have, I hope, developed a mastery of the highest secrets of life, happiness, and the means to protect and defend them.

"This undertaking has not been done in my self-interest. Indeed, that would run fundamentally counter to the teachings of Buddhism and humanism. No, Santiago, I am interested in the collective good. Greed insinuates itself into more greed: there is no vessel that can hold this vulgar spiral. This is the mistake that the monsters of history failed to learn, perhaps because they were slaves to their narcissistic psycho-pathologies. Perhaps it was because they were fools.

"Combining Zen meditation and martial arts, both of which test the extreme limits of human capability, Shaolin is perhaps the oldest style of Chinese martial arts. It originated and was developed in the Buddhist Shaolin temples nearly fifteen hundred years ago. It endures today. It is said, 'All martial arts under heaven originated from Shaolin.'

"The focus here is not about violence. What we seek is a state of readiness and complete awareness, only resorting to unquestionable definitive action when necessary.

"Most of these teachings and practices have been passed along by Buddhist monks. In Buddhism, wrathful deities are enlightened beings who take on wrathful forms in order to lead sentient lives. One might say that

Buddhists are pacifists, which is true. However, a pacifistic philosophy does not mean that one cannot take extraordinary action in combating those forces which intend harm, or the disruption of personal or global positive equilibrium. Yes, Buddhists can, and sometimes even should, defend themselves and people around them.

"However, consider this law: If you do it out of anger, you will suffer from the results of this anger. The key is to use violence without any negative feelings, but out of active compassion. If an attacker wants to kill not only you but also ten of your companions, less harm will be done if you kill him out of compassion towards your companions.

"You can also feel compassion for this attacker. Imagine how much he will suffer if he indeed commits his intended crimes! If you can stop him by defending yourself and your companions, thus saving him from torment, you definitely should do it.

"So, for example, if you were a specialist doctor who can save lives, your life should be protected. You or others should defend such a being for the sake of the patients who rely on the ability of that physician to heal.

"Here's another example. Imagine a mother defending her only child. She loves the child and she really doesn't mind spoiling her own karma. The only thing she wants is the safety and well-being of her beloved infant. She will resort to violence if this is the only way to protect the baby.

"Thus, Santiago, your intention to kill me will bring you bad karma. Worse, however, is the intention of your employer, Rex Donald: he intends to kill or suppress millions.

"This cannot be permitted.

"You know, Santiago, enlightenment can be achieved instantly by total awakening. It is possible. Let us hope that this door will open for you: the consequence for failing to walk through such an open door will result in your untimely death.

"I ask — what action will benefit the most people for the longest possible time? Compassion and unconditional love for others is the key.

"Why am I telling you all this, Santiago? You're a killer, sent to kill me. I have a wish that you will take a right action and re-direct yourself to eliminating a problem far greater and more threatening than me."

Dr. Marshall began to vigorously rub his exposed forearms. I understood fully that he was extremely powerful, but he was also a complex man with a real sense of integrity and ethics.

7

Assassination

Dr. Marshall continued in an orotund cadence: "Do you recall my mention of the Kennedy assassination?"

Of course I did. This was not a statement to be ignored.

Dr. Marshall stood and paced akimbo.

Suddenly a loud alarm went off as metal shutters rapidly dropped down from the ceiling, covering the massive glass window surround. As they lowered, I could see that a wave of missiles, launched from various locations, had been deployed on trajectories that all appeared to converge on the building we occupied.

A hidden panel in one of the rear walls slid open, revealing a large elevator.

Dr. Marshall shouted, "Get your ass in gear Santiago — *now!*"

The dozen bodyguards and aides who had been in attendance during our conversation rushed towards the elevator. With all of us safely inside, the doors shut and the elevator descended precipitously.

"So, Santiago," said Dr. Marshall, "you see this little chat we have been having is not bullshit. Rex Donald is making a pre-emptive attempt to silence me — and you!

"When we have retreated to more comfortable and safer quarters, I will tell you about what he has in mind for us all. We have prepared for this contingency. I had not planned on exposing you to our little secret hideaway, but now I have no choice.

"Our control center is about a mile below our mountain. It's hardened for an atomic attack. Hopefully, Rex Donald will not be stupid enough to use nukes, but with him, anything is possible. Insanity knows no limits."

After a nauseating ride lasting many minutes, the elevator opened. We faced a reinforced door like a bank vault. One of the guards punched in a security code and a steel door, eight feet thick, swung open. We entered a tunnel where a vacuum tube transport car awaited. All entered. The transport car, propelled by air pressure, accelerated at a neck-snapping rate. Several minutes later, we stopped at another vault door, and went through the same routine of code entry and access.

What I then saw is something never I'll never forget: A vast room hewn from the living rock, with hundreds of people sitting behind computer consoles, surrounded by enormous screens. Each set of screens was titled with different areas of focus: Military, Cyber, Banking, World Governments, Money Flows, Precious Metals, and so forth.

There was also a bank of screens displaying live images of every world leader, tracking them 'round the clock.

I heard a muffled boom and Dr. Marshall's subterranean command and control center shook slightly. We could see on the screens that a wave of massive jets, including stealth bombers and B-52s, soared high overhead. Many were being shot down by ground-based missiles, and they fell from the sky in lazy flaming arcs. We watched as one surviving bomber dropped a very large weapon — a Mother of All Bombs. The shock wave rolled over a large area including all of Santa Fe and its surrounding business and residential areas. Buildings were flattened, and in an instant the entire Santa Fe metropolitan area had been leveled: population, eighty thousand people.

From cameras mounted in the surrounding mountains, we saw that Dr. Marshall's mountaintop compound had been utterly demolished.

I turned to Dr. Marshall, who was nonchalant. It was, it seemed, simply the cost of doing his business. I remarked to Dr. Marshall that the underground cavern was amazing and unlike anything I had ever seen. A pretty penny, I bet!

"About fifty billion dollars each," he replied, with his eyes fixed on the screens. "We have several duplicated around the world. We are at war with global forces whose intention is to either kill or control the world population. Serious problems require serious responses!"

Dr. Marshall had, I surmised, been planning for this eventuality for years. It did not take a *summa cum laude* astrophysicist to understand that money was not an object.

"Our observation and control centers are linked by extensive underground transportation tubes," he continued. "These connect each facility to air strips one hundred miles from each. Through these tubes — from which the air has been evacuated — and traveling at four hundred miles per hour, we can reach our private airfields within twenty minutes.

"We expected 'Il Duce' Rex to pull something like this. We never doubted if; only when."

If President Rex Donald knew I was in Santa Fe to dispatch Dr. Marshall, he must have also realized that I would likely be annihilated along with Dr. Marshall. I was to have been just another pawn lost during the attack. However, I think he did not realize that such extreme preparations had been made to blunt his massive airborne assault.

"So," said Dr. Marshall, "now we should have a bit of supper and continue our discussions. The next moves on our global chessboard might not afford time to relax and finish our talks. You see, Santiago, I think when you realize that you have been sent here to finish me, you would also be a party to finishing humankind. I know you are an assassin, Santiago: but I also know about your life, the CIA, and your participation in covert operations. I'm betting that you will transcend your past and be cleansed in your own self-interest and in the interest of others.

"Interdiction to stop a purloined totalitarian march on humanity is serious business. I think you're up to that — we'll see. I do not cast aspersions lightly, but unless stopped, the despotic leaders of the two superpowers will fulfill their long-held dreams of genocide and unrepentant manifest destiny: a self-proclaimed entitlement to rule the planet.

"They are both psychopaths headed either for complete power or, failing that, terminal emotional aneurysm and awaiting straightjackets in rubber rooms. I want to shut the door on them both."

8

Extraordinary Times Require Extraordinary Action

Be the change you want to see in the world.
— **M.K. Gandhi**

I WAS A CAPTIVE in a world suddenly gone catawampus. I did not sign on for this.

Despite the dramatically violent events, Dr. Marshall was cool and unperturbed. Everything seemed to be expected, with no surprises.

He turned to me. "Look, Santiago, I want to take a little time to more deeply illuminate what forces are now at war. Our entire system of government has been suborned, purloined! The United States has a schizophrenic history: one the one hand, noble and good: the other side, imperialistic, genocidal, and domineering. We are here in the great Southwest. It is a repository, a virtual and actual concentration camp for those native Americans who were nearly wiped off the face of the earth. Let's not mince words: we are talking about genocide, ethnic cleansing, theft, and broken promises. The many tribes that were decimated had inhabited these lands for thousands of years. This is not a matter of conjecture: it is fact.

"The hubris of our founding fathers is remarkable. So, by the way, was their pursuit of finding a workable and just system of government. However, when one looks deeply into what actually occurred in the late 1700s, significant conflicts arose among the largely aristocratic and wealthy land and business owners who forged the structure we now call the United States.

"Our founders were largely slave owners. I can appreciate that the economic reality of the times weighed heavily in favor of maintaining that system, but the cruelty and disregard of fundamental human rights was overlooked, and remains so, even to this day.

"You may recall the race riots of the 1960s, and then in 1991 the police brutality presented in vivid video detail as Rodney King was beaten inhumanely by a half-dozen brazen Los Angeles police officers, who were then adjudged not guilty by a snowy white middle-class jury in the bigoted suburbs of Los Angeles. What followed was more race riots, deaths, and destruction — violence compounded with more violence.

"They want it that way: the more violence in the streets, the better the excuse for constructing a police state. This is a mechanism of deliberate tyranny.

"Benjamin Franklin, standing firm and tall with the Quakers; they were the only ones who decided to confront the early Congress with the wrongs inherent in slavery. Their decision was to put off resolution of this nasty question. Some sixty years later, this little delay tactic resulted in one of the most vicious civil wars ever fought.

"Teddy Roosevelt, whom I admire for his audacity, brilliance, and candor, had a ruthless streak which became manifest in the callous wars he waged in Cuba and the Philippines.

"Let us not confuse the myth of who we are with the reality.

"Were it not for George Washington's rejection of being appointed de facto king of America, we could well have ended with a representative government ultimately dominated by a royal and protected executive. In fact, despite the checks and balances embedded in the Constitution, the special powers invested in the executive stop just short of monarchy.

"The highest levels of governance are still dominated by the wealthy. Lawyers have written laws couched in incomprehensible jargon. This cannot be a mistake. Obscurity is a tangible form of suppression.

"I know I am hammering one nail after another in what we were all taught was a noble enterprise. I'll stop in just a bit. Forgive me for recollecting the painful side of our well-established history. It's important, however, to understand what pathways brought us to the unfortunate but inevitable present.

"When we see evil, it is essential to call it for what it is. Human beings, I have previously told you, are embedded with an inherent inability to see evil in others. I think it's based on self-protection. We are social creatures who want to see and believe that there is good in others.

"Only after being kicked, incontrovertibly and sometimes, often, do we finally react. Most folks, I believe, are decent: but many of us are infused with a proclivity towards manipulation, chicanery, and outright badness, typically linked to greed and anger. The Buddhists have known this for eons.

"Let me wrap here by pointing out that our justice system is accessible only to those with wealth, influence, and power. Why do you think our jails are filled to the brim with the socially, economically, and racially underprivileged? No other country in the world has incarcerated so many. More jails are built in the United States than schools!

"I have known, grown up with, and, for a significant portion of my life, been a part of this putrid conglomeration. I am ashamed of that. But my shame is not expressed by running away but by running *towards* and *against* what I know to be dead wrong. That's why we are here today, Santiago. It is no accident.

"Many parts of the world have realized that we have left the station of global responsibility, abandoning it for self-serving and strident purposes. If we cannot dominate, we annihilate. That has become our credo. We may not see it, but many do: they are unhappy. Revolted.

"Our inclination towards domination is not unique. Other titans share the same pathological and malignant disease for power. They have congealed and amassed, and are now making definitive and pre-emptive moves to solidify their grasp.

"We need to take these maniacs out of their oligarchy, which we once called democracy. Rex Donald is not the only one. He is not the root problem, but a symptom.

"The U.S. has a long but sordid history of imperialism, intrusion, greed, and a need to control. This does not discount our nobility or greatness. But it's important to realize that we, as a country, have engaged in a sustained march to control the planet: it started with slavery, enlarged with the genocide of the native population, and continued with the spread of manifest destiny, which did not end at the shores of California. We wanted it all.

"Many of us may have forgotten our sins, and instead we have taken shelter in self-congratulation for our proper engagement in struggles against evil, like the two world wars.

"We have also made it a habit to install dictators and strong men to do our bidding. We have bought our friends for alliances, which were primarily for our benefit.

"We have forgotten, but the world has not.

"Now that the orange orangutan, Rex Donald, is in the White House, the cat is out of the bag, and our friends, who once bowed before our powerful feet, are now openly laughing at the truth behind the Stars and Stripes.

"The game is over. We need to realize it and understand that that bullshit billionaire did not spring out of nowhere. He is the monster we created and deserve. While the majority of the public has been asleep at the wheel of both the Republican and Democratic Party bubble machines, the powerful have risen to new heights on both sides of the aisle.

"Do you think Bernie Sanders became a force from virtually out of nowhere? He is a kid out of the nineteen-sixties who rose to a position where his voice could be heard. He reminded us of the awesome responsibility of the social contract where a government is given power by the people, in exchange for making sure that our inalienable rights are preserved.

"Yes, the powerful shut him down. But that won't last. The throngs of us who remember the wrongs of Vietnam have not forgotten. They will not stay quiet while the very fabric of a just society continues to be ripped apart. It will take some time, but I pray a new breed is on its way to power. We need to support them, become them, finance them, and empower them.

"Too many of us bought the lie that the people we have elected really care about us, while they have turned around and betrayed fundamental notions of compassion and ethics. They care not for us! They have become intoxicated with power and have forgotten that there are real people who suffer terribly at their whims.

"We must remove them from power and put real people in charge. People with hearts and compassion. Not the lying, stupid, uneducated monsters we now have who have managed to hypnotize the increasingly uneducated with the outright deception that they really have the interests of the good of the people at heart. It's become a deadly game of show business. Showdown business.

"The audience may finally come to the realization that it's time to stop clapping. The emperor has no clothes!

"Some, like the Austrian-born British philosopher and economist Friedrich Hayek, have argued persuasively that society has been on a track towards totalitarianism, cloaked in the justification that central and consolidated control is in the interest of all. The will of a small minority has been imposed upon the people. The power of these minorities to act by taking money or property in pursuit of centralized goals destroys the rule of law and erodes individual freedoms.

"There is an increasing veneration for the state, the admiration of power, and of bigness for bigness's sake.

"It is believed that the successful use of competition as the principle of social organization precludes certain types of coercive interference, which is their justification and foundation for the exertion of authoritarian control.

"A just government has an implied duty to prevent fraud and deception, yet these mechanisms are essential to the ability to ply mind control of the collective unconscious. It is a nasty business that has become our daily business.

"Since the massive recovery of world stability in the 1950s, we have experienced a long-term plan to eliminate FDR's New Deal. They think it's a bad deal, and definitely not *their* deal. Banking controls have been largely eliminated in the interest of dominant powers who want to run unfettered; and, should they face trouble again, they will be blindly bailed out by the public on whose shoulders rests the ultimate responsibility for supporting their folly.

"We have seen this as recently as 2008, when the game, again, came to an abrupt stop. Crying that the world would collapse, billions of real and debt money — ultimately the responsibility of the public to repay — were pumped into the greedy hands and pockets of the power elite. Real people experienced no real relief. Homes were stolen, careers ruined, and peaceful lives with the hope of a secure landing decimated.

"Those engineers of greed are now in power, both economically and governmentally. Adding to this morass is the reality that nuclear technology is no longer in the hands of one or two, but many. They are collectively able to incinerate the globe without notice.

"So, Santiago, that is the short story of why Rex Donald and Anton Milonov are making their checkmate move to close down the game with exquisite finality.

"You were sent here, not to kill me, but to kill off human kind. You will not succeed; I think you know that.

"*They* will not succeed: I know that."

9

The Agony of Santiago

"Dr. Marshall," I said, "we've just been attacked. Don't you think that immediate action should be taken? Why are we headed to your private dining room here a mile below the surface of the earth?"

"Santiago," he replied coolly, "a global response has been underway since those planes approached my mountain. As the French say, *"Les jeux sont faits."*

"Sorry, my French is a bit rusty."

"The die is cast. The bets are placed and cannot be changed. The game is in motion. The great and unstoppable forces of nature are speeding ahead. Fate awaits."

"One cannot be a pacifist in the face of evil."

"Shit."

Dr. Marshall was making perfect sense. I had met Rex Donald through fellow operatives at the CIA. His father, Arnold, the New York slumlord tycoon, had been connected to the Agency for years. Arnold Donald had dispatched many of my colleagues on clandestine missions. Most of us in the CIA, who did not turn double agent, derived a substantial income from highly paid moonlighting. Arnold Donald was a frequent client of mine, usually wanting someone or another out of his way.

Dr. Marshall's father was an active client. These were men who respected no boundaries and had no sense of right or wrong.

The world can be your oyster if you have the proper tools to pry open even the most resistant shells. The CIA had quite a bag of tools from which we could draw, including traditional and biological weapons.

The toys of the James Bond movies fall far short of what we actually have in our arsenal. The public is kept largely unaware, except when various experimental materials leech into the ground water or escape from carefully concealed laboratories infecting the atmosphere.

We point accusingly to the German Holocaust, when in fact the United States Government has been responsible for massive population "control and eradication." This is not information generally appreciated or known to the public, but we have, for quite some time, the tools to overtly or covertly wipe the planet clean of animal and human life many times over.

I lived it. I've seen it. I've used it.

The mission President Rex Donald had dispatched me to perform was relatively straightforward, or so I believed. In reality, it was anything but.

I'm in my sixties. In good shape. I'm told that I have the appearance of a rich man: refined and, dare I say, elegant.

I don't see myself that way. But others do, so there might be something to it.

My outwardly sophisticated appearance has enabled me to gain easy access to high circles. I'm a thug, but I don't look like one.

Operating in stealth has always been an attribute which has allowed easier access to political bigwigs, private clubs, and rich women willing to fall into bed with an exotic stranger.

Women who are powerful or are married to the powerful are often lonely and want to soften the torment of their isolation. You could think of me as a kind of Caesar Romero — an available Latin lover.

Often valuable secrets spring forth concurrent with expertly performed cunnilingus or the spasm of orgasm. This was the basis of my meeting with Rex Donald: his wife and I had been hot for years. She was a trophy, a statuesque beauty who loved to conjugate, and I don't mean her verbs.

Fortunately, she was married to a man whose sole interest in life was to fuck others — but not in the carnal sense.

Mrs. Rex, as I thought of her, loved to wear garter belts, silk stockings, high heels, Cartier earrings: and nothing else. Exactly my style.

Interesting, too, that I had a similar sexual connection with Dr. Marshall's wife subsequent to her divorce from him. She was a whore as much as he was a nobleman.

I loved fucking them both and they loved fucking me. Life is short.

Dr. Marshall had married Anika before he had found his true self. They met while he was ambassador to Russia, appointed by Bush II. He was not always enlightened and had played with the trappings of luxury and sequin-gowned women.

Anika was a quintessential Russian stunner. Her accent was hypnotic; it made me think of warm French Calvados. Her lips were unforgettable, and when she spoke, I only wanted to suck on her scrumptious mouth, her breasts — every part of her.

When Rex learned that I was involved with both his wife and Dr. Marshall's Anika, he was actually pleased that someone was servicing his lady. He had grown impotent from greed. He was not a man. He was a unilaterally directed machine.

What did interest Rex, then a New York-based real estate mogul, was that my tangential involvement with Dr. Marshall was made possible through his wife.

Rex Donald, before and after he became president, was obsessed, as he had always been, with Dr. Marshall.

He knew Dr. Marshall was brilliant and wealthy as half of humanity. He also knew, from their early years together, that Dr. Marshall, given the chance, would neuter him. Rex Donald feared Dr. Marshall, and with good reason.

My first assignment from Rex Donald (for which I earned $10 million!) was to garrote the lovely Anika. I did so as part of a sexual play ritual that went deliberately too far.

Donald wanted to inflict pain on Dr. Marshall, and crushing his former wife's windpipe seemed, to him, like a good way to exact some level of revenge. Though divorced, Dr. Marshall had two children with Anika; for their sake, the estranged couple maintained contact and maintained a semblance of civility. It was probably for show, but I can't say for sure.

So, having Dr. Marshall's wife viciously killed was an attractive ploy that Rex Donald rather enjoyed. When I reported to him about the outcome, he danced a jig.

He was, and is, a very bad man. While I too am bad, I take no pleasure in it. He does.

Rex Donald's interest in me went further than taking revenge by killing Dr. Marshall's former spouse. He realized that the closer I could get to Dr. Marshall, the easier it would be for me to deal a final blow to his nemesis. Rex Donald had deliberate motives for everything he planned and did. These are some of the real characteristics of a psychopath.

From my tender whispered conversations with Anika, pillow to pillow, I had found out where Dr. Marshall was living and a good deal about his very private life.

Rex Donald, now president of the United States, had paid me well to share with him all that I learned. I did.

Not only did I betray the living, I also betrayed the dead.

I don't think President Donald knew that Dr. Marshall was so far advanced in his plans to counteract Donald's own Machiavellian intentions: the president's plans to actualize world domination in partnership with his dear friend, President Anton Molinov of Russia.

Clearly, though, he had to know that Dr. Marshall had enormous resources at his disposal and the ability and intent to use them.

The elimination of Anika was concealed by my former colleagues at the CIA. The crime scene was thoroughly cleansed. Suspicion never fell on me: the silence of the Justice Department, FBI, and local police were all bought and paid. Absolute power corrupts absolutely.

I had asked myself, why was President Donald so concerned about Dr. Marshall? I knew that he had hated him for years. But there had to be something more, much more.

President Rex Donald was deeply afraid of Dr. Marshall. This far exceeded, it seemed to me, a conventional life-long mutual dislike and distrust. These were powerful people. They hate for real reasons, and while they may be capricious, typically something very material is operative.

After the fatal completion of my affair with Anika, I endeavored to dig into this more deeply. I had gotten down with vicious dogs: I was bound to rise with fleas.

When one has access to the CIA infrastructure, nearly anything about anyone can be revealed. The level of surveillance of everyday people, let alone the special and powerful, is beyond comprehension. The government keeps collected information, drawn from many sources, consolidated into comprehensive databases, under the control of the military, the police, and the NSA.

A few well-placed individuals — friends of mine — opened those access points willingly and without question. A few hundred thousand dollars fully facilitated my access to the information I sought.

"Santiago, you seem to be lost in space," said Dr. Marshall. "We've just sat down for dinner and you have disconnected. Regrets, perhaps?"

Dr. Marshall had caught me as I had been lost in thought. More importantly, he arrested my recollection of the urgent question I had sought to answer, now months ago, before this clandestine mess turned bad.

The question: Why? What had made Rex Donald so paralyzed with fear?

Dr. Marshall had told me their fathers were "friends"— read, "mobsters." The joining of the Russian and American oligarchs began, in earnest, and then was realized at first with the coalesced agenda that enabled the assassination of President John F. Kennedy.

The two fathers, Arnold Donald and Norman Marshall, were prime movers in this toxic game of global chess. Their sons had carried on their father's ignominious legacies: Rex Donald embarked on an evil path, while Dr. James Marshall took a turn, eventually towards the good.

Who would checkmate the other?

I had inadvertently climbed into their steel cage of ultimate global confrontation.

10

A Dirty Business

"YOU ARE NOT eating — what gives?" asked Dr. Marshall.

We were seated in an elegantly appointed dining room, with waiters impeccably dressed in starched white jackets and crisp black bow ties. Such an unlikely setting a mile deep into Dr. Marshall's mountain.

A man in a leather coat, one of the same who fingered me in the Santa Fe bar, approached Dr. Marshall, leaned over, and spoke with cupped hand over Dr. Marshall's ear.

Dr. Marshall remained reserved. His facial expression did not betray any emotion. He was the ultimate in cool, deliberate, meditative — piercingly sharp.

He turned to me. "Santiago, President Rex Donald has just declared martial law. The Constitution is suspended and the civil rights of our entire population have been put on ice. In response, most all world leaders have done the same. The Russians, Chinese, and other totalitarian leaders have long since squeezed their iron fist over their vast populations. Many already exert absolute control over their military and national infrastructures. No need to repeat what is already done.

"They are acting in precisely the harmony and cooperation we expected. They have moved towards solidifying absolute control over every living soul.

"No surprises here!

"Now, back to you, Santiago. You see, I know you killed my former wife. I can't say that I am heartbroken over that. What does disturb me is that you robbed my children, for better or worse, of their mother. While she turned out to be a beautiful, beguiling and an evil witch, she was still the mother of my kids. If your spouse, former or otherwise, were so dispatched, what would you do? Hey?"

I could not duck such a question, and given the impossibility of any escape, I defaulted to something which does not come easily to me: honesty.

"Well, I would not rest until that wrong had been righted!"

"Good, Santiago, then it should not bother you that your wife, children, grand kids, brothers and sisters are now all sleeping with the fishes! They're all dead. I've only spared you because you may yet be useful to us. That will be your choice. Now we truly have something in common. Like it?"

Enraged but caged, I could feel blood rush into my face. I wanted to vomit, but would not give Dr. Marshall the satisfaction that he had indeed broken me and taken the little bit of sweetness remaining in my life.

The man seated across the table from me was every bit as ruthless as I have ever been. He had proclaimed himself to be spiritually enlightened, but he had also been clear that for every action there is an equal or opposite reaction. Evil, in his playbook, would not stand unopposed — ever.

"You do realize that Rex Donald is a mobster?" he said. "He is surrounded by mobsters dressed in five-thousand-dollar suits, many educated at Harvard, advanced degrees, and the trappings of refinement; but at the end of the day, they are mobsters in sheep's clothing. They are pigs.

"Sure, they order hits in the old fashioned way, the old Brooklyn snap brim fedora way; but they have also refined their game. They use information to exert power and control. It is their ultimate weapon and they have been masterful. You know that, Santiago.

"Both Rex Donald's father and mine built their fortunes on blackmail and extortion, on murder, on transcending the rule of law. Who needs legislated law when you can make your own?

"The question is, who is the *capo de capo*? Who is the don behind the don? Interesting question, don't you think? Who is the Rex behind the Rex?

"You see, the power elite who are now rising to world domination are nothing more than gutter slime: stinking, cheap, illiterate punks. I despise them and so should you."

Where was Dr. Marshall headed? He was now fully animated and emotionally, passionately involved. His demeanor was still elegant, but he was engaged, even enraged. That much was plain.

"They are gleefully ringing their jingoistic bells," he continued. "Remember the Hitler Youth rallies? If you intend to distract attention from your own monstrous actions, point to others. Bad guys need to have an enemy. It matters not if such an enemy has to be created. The new Jews are the Islamic fundamentalists, the gays, the immigrants — whomever are ripe for suppression and castigation.

"You see, Santiago, in each one of us lies a monster in wait — genetically embedded and, given proper circumstances, ready to unleash fury. I may have become a Buddhist master, but my fundamental make-up, like yours, lingers. Like you, sitting here passively now, we have the instant potential to set free the vehemence that lies within.

"I've have just killed off all who are near and dear to you. We won't test the waters to see what you would do if I put a gun or knife in your hands; my associates would instantly cut your head off, but for a split second you would have enjoyed a sweet moment of revenge. Don't get excited, I'm playing with you.

"How many of us humans have died blindly laboring under the illusion that the ultimate price was worth paying? The Germans frozen stiff in the Russian winter; the Yankees and the Southern rebels facing each other down, gun barrel to gun barrel, in what was certain extermination; the troops of the First World War living in muddy holes sucking mustard gas! For what?

"From where does such blind obedience spring? From stupidity and a misinformed belief that we are transcendent from the reality of mortality?

"I'm not quite sure, Santiago, but I think it might have something to do with servile obedience. It may be some kind of mechanism in which we invest and subsume our very lives to the will of others. The ultimate sacrifice — for what? The belief that there is something beyond our precious lives? Altruism? God will take care of us, regardless? Do you buy that?

"Whatever the explanation, the mechanism of self-sacrifice seems to have spanned our time as a species.

"I promised you some background about how I became the man I am now.

"To do that requires a bit of historical recollection. I think we have the time and I think it might be helpful for you to understand my often twisted and tortured journey, a trip that has brought me to the conclusion that, in the war between the dark and the light, the light must prevail: at any cost.

"Aristotle referred to this kind of natural imperative as the need to *be*: the necessity that an acorn grows into a tree. The French philosopher Henri Bergson described these dialectic forces as *"elan vital,"* the vital force by which even a tender blade of grass can burst through cement, seeking life-giving light: the natural obligation to become, to be alive, to fulfill the implicit wish of nature."

Dr. Marshall was again approached by one of his lieutenants. Another hushed exchange. This time Dr. Marshall smiled, fully.

11

Lessons

"LET'S TALK ABOUT the Mob," said Dr. Marshall. "The Mob is not a thing, a word; it is an understanding. Whether implicit or explicit, it is a belief that consolidated power is an entitlement vested in a few — a sanctioned few. The rest of us are simply pieces on the board of life to be moved: obediently.

"I'd like to tell you about how I was appointed ambassador to Russia. To paint this picture, we will need to go back to pour the foundation that led to my appointment. It is a story couched in infamy.

"I mentioned that my father was involved in uranium — in Australia, Canada, and Kazakhstan. Following his involvement with Oppenheimer and the development of the first atomic bomb, he knew that whoever controlled the supply of radioactive minerals would gain incontrovertible power to source what he correctly predicted was a grab by world powers to successfully duplicate the product of Los Alamos. He was right.

"During the Second World War, the Germans, the Russians, and the Japanese were all racing, at varying levels of effort, to make the ultimate weapon. However, such a massive undertaking required considerable resources: money, scientists, football fields of factories, and the concentration to pointedly focus. It also required the very slow and cumbersome process of extracting plutonium from uranium ore.

"Hitler knew that the possession of an atomic weapon would have led to certain world dominance. Hell, he had nearly achieved this, and stopped just short of overtaking England, halted only by the brute determination of the British and a nasty body of water called the English Channel. The British, to their credit, had developed an early form of radar. They could electronically anticipate airborne invasions. Brilliant.

"It is also not often discussed that the Germans did attack the United States — militarily, which was symbolic and significant. The mass mind control programs of our government have consistently downplayed this reality. Can you imagine the panic which would have ensued if those several forays were known to the public?

"To make matters worse, Hitler, mired in his unbridled hatred of the Jews, killed, exiled, or forced the most brilliant of their Jewish scientists from Germany.

"Please remember that it was Einstein's thought experiment which led to realizing that matter was equivalent to energy. If a means could be realized to unleash that energy, the world would be changed, forever.

"Einstein fled his native land, as did many others, leaving the Germans with a paucity of talent.

"Hitler was obsessed with destroying the British, and he nearly succeeded. Rockets became his fixation: annihilate the Brits, and the pathway to the takeover of America was within reach. It was Hitler's version of Germany's manifest destiny and their perceived prerogative to control the world. The creation of a global Third Reich and a thousand-year plan for Aryan supremacy.

"But sociopaths are not rational. They are unable to see or listen. This kind of ignorance ultimately leads to downfall. In the case of Adolph, his psychopathology was a blessing.

"The Russians were besieged: not only were they fighting for their lives within miles of Moscow, but the insane Stalin was also busy exterminating millions of his own people. He feared them and their potential to rise up against the brutality of his unrelenting, vicious, and unquestionably powerful dictatorship.

"The Japanese were under siege and their base of natural resources limited. Despite their intrusion into China, they did not possess the material necessary to fight for their lives while simultaneously mastering atomic weaponry.

"The Sicilian mob has had a deep history. Sicily had been invaded and conquered numerous times throughout the millennium, alternately being subjugated by one foreign power or another. To counter this changing landscape of external interference, an ex-officio government arose: the Mafia, the Cosa Nostra, the family. They took over the governance of all things, including local disputes, decisions over territory, and economics: in short, anything having to do with daily life, survival, and crime.

"Their bond was blood and wherever necessary, unrepentant violence. This was not a game. Their credo was and remains based on absolute obedience.

"The roots of the Mafia may have been boutique at first, but when they gained control over all of Italy and infiltrated most of Europe, their growing appetite for power was fed by the continuing success of their efforts. This included the control of the Church and its massive, world-encompassing economic empire, banks, and mastery of mind control.

"In the late 1800s and early 1900s, they skipped over the Atlantic onto American soil. The land of plenty. The land of opportunity. A land waiting to be had.

"It was Mario Gentile who was the master of masters: *capo de capos*. At first, in the United States, they operated piecemeal — a gang here, a family there, a racket in booze, drugs, whores, protection, all small but increasingly lucrative.

"Follow the money, Santiago. If you want to get to the truth, always follow the money. But money without power is like a gun without bullets. You need both to have a real weapon.

"As the reach of the Mafia extended, little stood in their way: judges and police could be bought, elections rigged, puppets installed in governments, appointments of captive goons in the military — you get it, right? A march towards unfettered power. That drive has not abated.

"But violence is messy. Unpopular. Often times, too spectacular: gunned-down bodies in the middle of Manhattan or Los Angeles, mass murders in Chicago, slaughters in New Orleans. The public gets nervous as they feel their lives become encroached. They demand counter measures. Who wants to live in a world where the domestic tranquility of daily life becomes threatened by whimsical violence unleashed at any time?

"As the power of the Mob grew and their wealth amassed, a slow and deliberate transition had begun. The old-time gangsters were eliminated through rival wars, increasing police intervention, prosecution, and imprisonment. Most of the bootleggers and pimps faded from ostentatious and cavalier notoriety. Only the quiet forces behind them survived.

"While most of the thugs were killed off or incarcerated, their hidden and most powerful enforcers cemented: the founding credo of Mario Gentile survived and thrived.

"His buddy, Meyer Lansky, died peacefully in his eighties, in own bed. Sure, the government tried to nail him, but his world-reaching global power and connections afforded him ultimate protection. Lansky was the chief economist of the gang, now spread out to include numerous nationalities, business enterprises and ethnic backgrounds.

"During the Second World War, Lansky even became an operative of the Office of Naval Intelligence, and mounted numerous anti-Nazi attacks in concert with, and with the blessing of the United States government. The lines drawn between the good and bad are faint.

"Most of Lansky's massive wealth was secretly transferred to secret Swiss bank accounts, where it remains hidden to this day. He was, in coordination with the Sicilian mob, the Accountant: the moneyman who straddled the underworld and the government.

"One other ditty: Lanksy was born in Russia. His birth name was Meier Suchowlanski. Remember that, Santiago. Lansky was a Russian Jew born in Belarus.

"Other thugs included such notorious figures as Joseph P. Kennedy Sr., father of John F. Kennedy. Joe Kennedy ran booze from around the world, taking full advantage of the absurdity of Prohibition. Instead of inheriting a criminal legacy, he became known as an investor, a businessman, a movie-maker, a lady's man, and a politician: a Boston Brahmin.

"Make no mistake, Joe Kennedy was a slug from the underworld who smoothly transitioned into legitimate society and saw to it that many of his prized brood received the ultimate mantle of legitimacy — Harvard educations underpinned by unfathomable wealth.

"No need to be overtly nasty: too much publicity, too many problems. Why continue to be labeled as a social pariah when you can don the cloak of complete respectability?

"So the old Mafia, now with global tentacles, reached into nearly every world government and institution. Money has been one of their indisputable measures of success. Hence the invasion of Wall Street, government on all levels, banks, insurance companies, pawn shops, check cashing, gun running, construction, ship building, armaments, unions: the list of the infiltrated infrastructure and institutions of the planet is unlimited.

"Santiago, if you were to play this scenario out to a logical conclusion, would you want to include nuclear stockpiles to your portfolio?

"That's when my father and Arnold Donald, together, made their move to control the world supply of nuclear ore. In the 1940s, Kazakhstan was an incorporated part of the emerging Soviet Union. It is the home to some of the largest deposits of uranium. My father and Arnold Donald had bought these mines, and their monopoly reached around the globe to also include Canada and Australia, home to more vast amounts of the killer mineral.

"Although plutonium 239 is present in most minerals, having been formed billions of years ago by supernova explosions, it is particularly well-concentrated in uranium, to the tune of two to four parts per million. To get to enough of the radioactive component, it's necessary to have massive extraction techniques that can efficiently process millions of tons of ore. This requires enormous expense and machinery. The prize: global power.

"I certainly don't discount the importance of biological weapons. The Mob has their claws dug into those, too. But the simplicity of a nuclear bomb can neatly dispose of millions: quickly. Deploying such a weapon is relatively simple, whereas the use of biologics, though achievable, is a good deal more problematic. This is an esoteric digression, but important to keep in mind.

"Fast forward to Cuba in the early days of the Kennedy Administration and the showdown with Russia. The Soviets were actively setting up nuclear launch sites ninety miles from Florida. Kennedy's Bay of Pigs, a badly bungled attempt to seize back control of Cuba from Soviet-friendly Castro, had blown apart, tragically involving the loss of many lives, given for nothing.

Kennedy was under pressure from the Mob to regain the hold they had lost in Cuba. Their exile from the island had cost the Mafia billions of dollars: their safe haven was outside the reach of the U.S. authorities, and came with the ability to operate with impunity. The "boys" were not happy.

"Of course, the business dealings of my father and Arnold Donald would not be affected by the discontinuation of the Russian nuclear buildup in Cuba, as the world continued to satisfy its insatiable appetite to construct nuclear stockpiles. Nikita Khrushchev, Stalin's next in line, was a bombastic alcoholic, drunk with his new-found power and willing to force the potential of a global conflagration.

"He was also tied in with the Mob. His national interests were conflicted, as were Kennedy's. However, their personal interests were not.

"They both worked for the same boss: The *capo de capo*, a descendant of Mario Gentile. Incidentally and somewhat humorously, "gentile" means "polite" in Italian. An interesting twist on words, hey? Nothing polite about any of it.

"Both Kennedy and Khrushchev and their long line of political successors on either side of the world do *not* have *real* national affiliations or loyalties. They are loyal to themselves and to a transnational oligarchy in the new world order: an order which transcends the illusion of nationality, political parties, and affiliations.

"A concept which ignores global responsibility and governance.

"Nationalism is a painful delusion: a distraction from the real agenda. A good way to keep this ruse alive is through finger-pointing, posturing, misleading differences in political beliefs, self-serving military buildups, and manufactured imperialistic encroachments.

"This is all sound and fury, signifying nothing. But through mass mind control techniques, premised heavily on the works of Edward Bernays, a cousin of Sigmund Freud, methods for controlling the collective mind have become more refined as information sources have consolidated into pinpoint accuracy: the ownership of the global media has concomitantly fallen into the hands of a few powerful corporations. Their agendas are linked to the will of the Mob.

"The biggest and most powerful economic engine we possess, in this country, is feeding and building the military. The same is true with Russia: their primary business is military and energy. Save those Russian specialties, their economy has never included anything in the interest of their population. Probably never will.

"Were it not for the New Deal in the United States — FDR's curative gift to a broken society and the lip service paid to the public through Social Security programs, infrastructure buildup, and so forth — the United States would have, long ago, ignored the needs of the people and broken an assumed social contract in which the people transferred power to the government in exchange for the free pursuit of liberty and happiness. A bad joke riddled with broken-down promises.

"The manifestation, the measure of the disintegration of a great social concept, has become abundantly clear: What we have now is the outright invasion of all branches of the government by Mob-based interests and actors. The thugs of old are now re-enacting their fundamental predisposition. Though dressed to kill, they have surfaced to again talk and act like the thugs they have always been. Their pretension of niceties has been set aside. Why bother with pretext?

"The presumed integrity and dignity presumed by our aristocratic founders has been replaced by Wall Street power brokers. The nouveau Mafia no longer see the need to perpetrate the illusion of civility.

"The old order which prolonged the distortion of legitimacy is dying off by the day. Rex Donald is one of the perpetrators of this degradation, but he is not the only one.

"Khrushchev and Kennedy were, amazingly, allies. Their interests were tied to the Mob. The Mob's interests were tied to my father's and Donald's. They were all one and the same.

"Kennedy had blown a promise he made to the Mob. Retake Cuba, get it back. He blew it. Concurrently, Bobby Kennedy, now attorney general, turned on the will of his father and went after the unions, Jimmy Hoffa, and the Chicago political power machine who all had been bought to elect Kennedy president by an historically slim margin.

"Idealistic Bobby betrayed them: they wanted revenge. They wanted to exact their pound of flesh by taking the life of the president.

"Khrushchev was happy to oblige. Through the KGB, they tapped Lee Harvey Oswald, a former U.S. soldier turned Russian sympathizer to take the fall. They also tapped other CIA and Russian operatives, operating in a carefully interlaced fashion to realize the plot.

"Khrushchev had the full support of the Mob, who had hoped that with Kennedy removed, they would have a chance at retaking Cuba and reinvigorating their nuclear intentions pointed at the United States. But Castro was a rough customer and deflected several of Kennedy's assassination attempts, some of which nearly succeeded. These efforts were sponsored and shepherded by the Mob, who used Kennedy and the government.

These plots failed. Kennedy had to go. He fucked up.

"Everyone was played against each other. No rules: whoever emerged from the chaos alive would be the winner."

"My father and Donald senior coordinated JFK's assassination with Luigi Gentile and Khrushchev. To make sure that the truth behind this ultimate, history-altering plot never surfaced, a few things were set in place. With the cooperation of the Dallas police, Jack Ruby, a Chicago-born Jew with parental roots in Poland and Russia, was deployed. The cops were paid to look the other way as Ruby walked, armed, into the tunnel where Oswald was being led away for further interrogation and the real possibility of spilling the truth. This could not be allowed.

"So yet another person with Russian roots has entered the picture — this time to silence the apparent perpetrator of the assassination. I have it on good authority that the other agents who shot Kennedy from the knoll, facing the presidential motorcade, were spirited out of the country and died, in obscurity, in Siberia.

"That left the controlling elite to deal with the Presidential Commission appointed by the new President, Lyndon Johnson, another pigeon of the Mob. This was not so easy; they were dealing with apparently impeccable figures of the legitimate establishment including the chief justice of the United States, Earl Warren, a former governor of California, with an unapproachable reputation of integrity. But, big money buys big favors!

"Backed by Khrushchev, Johnson, and the Mob, Earl Warren and friends cloaked the truth in a massive report of the assassination, interwoven with obfuscation and chicanery. But they carried the imprimatur of infallibility and legitimacy, although now, fifty-plus years later, few accept their findings.

"The forensics were indisputable: no lone shooter here. Gone were Oswald, Ruby (who in 1967 died of lung cancer while in jail awaiting retrial), no collaboration from the protected co-conspirators, no admission by Khrushchev or Johnson. It was left to the public to muddle through force-fed garbage: after all, would the government lie about the murder of the most popular president in the history?

"As for Lyndon Johnson, a Texas television station operator turned master political manipulator, quickly fashioned the concept of the Great Society: admirable, but flawed. It was a brilliant distraction. He was a penultimate political magician. The vision for the Great Society, it is true, gave birth to Medicare and other great social programs aimed at improving the societal good, but it came at a price.

"While instituting these programs, Johnson was also embroiled with Vietnam, an increasingly bloody, expensive, and needless slaughter. How could he pay for building the Great Society while simultaneously fighting an expensive overseas war? There simply were not enough funds generated from the tax base to finance these endeavors. Assuming massive debt was not then considered a good alternative — as it is now! Kick the can and let the working class eventually pick up the pieces, sometime in the future when the thieves are long gone.

"Remember, too, Santiago, that billions were made by military contractors: war is good for business, at least some businesses.

"The solution to Johnson's problem was to steal the Social Security Trust Fund. The trillions needed to support these immensely costly enterprises, war and peace, lay with tapping into the vast sums built up in Social Security

— a heretofore sacred fund established in the wake of the Great Depression by Franklin Delano Roosevelt, a New York powerhouse with a sense of social right, and his principled wife, Eleanor.

"I have been the trustee of numerous trusts, and I know that breaking or misusing funds insulated by numerous legal protections is a very dangerous and complicated enterprise. But Johnson figured a way — he was that good.

"Nixon, another monster manipulator, helped to complete the process, later to be toyed with again and again by a government inclined, *at any cost,* to continue to insure the perceived viability and reliability of the full faith and credit of the United States.

"FDR had made a mistake by not originally designating the Social Security fund as a *trust.* They instead called it an *account,* which could be mingled with the general operating budget of the country. Later, a series of complicated rules were instituted, nearly incomprehensible, which designated what funds were protected and which were not. It gets complicated. But complication was convenient and confusing.

"The confusion allowed Johnson to access billions in Social Security funds, which were specifically intended to protect the population from ever again suffering the indignities and poverty resulting from the overheated twenties.

"So, Johnson transferred the assets of Social Security into the general operating budget. This gave him enough funds to wage war and build Medicare. Please remember that Medicare was originally conceived to protect those who could not protect themselves. The public grew increasingly unhappy with the special treatment afforded to the poor and wanted these entitlements for themselves:

hence, as long as anyone one survives through sixty-five, they are able to tap into a fund originally intended for the poorest. Greed!

"The Mob-dominated insurance cartel also wanted to stick their hands in that pot of gold. The bigger the Federal program, the more there was for them to steal. They bought their way through continuous "campaign financing" to do just that: the representative government became completely controlled and beholding to corporate money — read *Mob* money!

"So, you see the checks and balances contemplated, with a degree of real nobility, by the likes of Jefferson, Hamilton, Washington, and Madison have been steadily disappearing in plain view. A sleeping public has gotten exactly what their slumber deserves: robbery in the guise of democracy. Democracy is a dying concept: has been for a long time. It is now in a final death rattle. Can you hear it, Santiago?

"My father and Arnold Donald enabled the assassination of Kennedy and they financed the cover-up. They did it at the behest and with the full participation of the Mafia and the governments they now controlled.

"The payback my father arranged for me was exacted from George H. W. Bush. You will, of course, remember, that he was once director of the CIA. Funny how the spies take control of governments. I was appointed U.S. Ambassador to Russia, as much as a political favor, as to keep an eye on the family business and to do the bidding of the Mob.

"So, I was no choir boy.

"While I was in Russia, Anika, a Russian operative, was sent to seduce me. She was irresistible. I was sucker-punched. I was an idiot. My little head ruled me. I paid the price.

"Now you may have a better idea of who you fucked and how my own family has been an active participant with the Mob — a Mob no longer needing to operate *sub-rosa*. Welcome to the world of Donald, Molinov, and Luigi Gentile, great grandson of the Gentile clan: now de facto White House chief of staff.

"These are the scum who wield ultimate powers."

12

Gloves Off

DINNER WAS FINISHED. I had barely eaten.

"I think it's time for sleep." Dr. Marshall sarcastically rolled his eyes and chuckled dismissively while looking at me, mouth pinched slightly. "It's late and tomorrow will be a big day."

He had made his point. The gravity of history as he knew it had been well stated. Dr. Marshall was a monumental intellect: studied, fabulously well informed, really quite astounding and frightening. He also had a vision of the future and the means to realize it.

"My associates will escort you to your quarters," he continued. "I am sure you will be comfortable. Pardon the full-body cavity search, but we've come way too far to take any chances. I have plans for you."

His guards marched me down a long hallway, opened the door to a beautifully appointed suite, searched me as promised, and instructed me that I would be monitored with sensors, television cameras, and unannounced visits.

It was made clear to me that if I made any attempt to escape or pull a trick, a paralytic gas would be pumped into the room, rendering me totally unconscious. Fair warning.

I bathed and collapsed into a dreamless sleep. Nothing left to dream. Just emptiness. I think that's what Dr. Marshall intended.

The next morning, his associates unlocked the door. Dr. Marshall stood behind them, dressed in saffron-colored monk's robes, his head now clean shaven: his skin glowing, his aura radiating a golden light.

A magnificent Mozart piano concerto poured from invisible speakers, surrounding us all. It was to be a new day: a day like none other I had ever spent.

13

A Blissful Search

"PLEASE SANTIAGO, FOLLOW me."

We walked, side by side, down a long, tubular tunnel. The elevated platform floor was carpeted in a plush red deep pile. The surrounding tube was uniformly lit with smooth, soft light.

We arrived at a threshold: two golden doors, each of which bore a duplicate, raised transcription: โอม มณิ ปทฺเม หฺมฺ – *On Main Padme Hūw.* I did not ask Dr. Marshall for a translation — I had a good idea what lay beyond.

Dr. Marshall's associates ceremoniously and in unison each opened a door. We entered a large globe-shaped room, a kind of bubble floating in space. A muted, warm purple light uniformly illuminated this simple yet magnificent place. There is something about pure simplicity that speaks of eternity.

The red silk carpet of the hallway extended into the global chamber. On a black carved onyx lotus sat a brilliantly detailed statue of a golden Buddha — in silent and perfect repose.

There is something about the smile of a flawless Buddha: knowing, kind, amused, thoughtful — gentle. This Buddha was faultless.

Two black meditation cushions were precisely placed before the statue.

"Santiago, this is Buddha Shakyamuni: you are not required or expected to believe or accept anything. There are no conditions attached. No reverence is required. Just silence.

"If you learn anything: take it with you. If you learn nothing: take that with you.

"Now, join me for a few silent moments. Here, sit, and cross your legs like mine. Be comfortable, back straight, eyes forward, hands rested on your knees, thumb and first finger lightly touching. Place your tongue on the back of your upper teeth: it will relax your *chi*, your life force and, incidentally, your salivation will slow but your oral cavity will not become dry. It's an ancient secret."

Side by side, we sat. It was comforting yet very strange for me. I had never been in such a setting before. The realization that this man had ordered the execution of my entire family, my legacy, my dearest ones, was a thought I could not put aside. Yet, I could understand that a certain justice had been exacted. I had killed and he had killed. We had developed a certain comradeship, one made in the wake of an aborted assassination attempt.

Dr. Marshall spread his saffron robes carefully before his feet: respectful and silent. The aesthetics of perfection were important: they were a symbol of pure fidelity. Dr. Marshall closed his eyes, breathed deeply through his nostrils and, for all appearances, sunk into bliss. I tried to do the same, but my mind ricocheted between one random thought and another.

"Santiago," he said, "some require a lifetime to quiet the mind. Just return to your breath each time your mind wanders. Your breath is your life force: keep it going. Stop breathing and you are gone. Return to your breath."

I did as he suggested. My scattered thoughts slowed as I returned to my breath, breathing in, breathing out. Sinking, slowly sinking into a place of pure safety and comfort: amazing.

I could sense the guards standing watch behind us. They never left Dr. Marshall's side: never.

After what seemed to be a period of infinite silence, I sensed a very slight movement. One of the guards had moved a step closer to Dr. Marshall. Instantly, Dr. Marshall emerged from his profound meditative state, and in one completely fluid, choreographed motion leapt to his feet and kicked the head of his guard with a ferocious chop. I heard the guard's neck snap, and as he fell to the floor, a trickle of blood oozed from his mouth. He was dead.

"We have known for some time that one of my men had been paid by Rex Donald to dispose of me," said Dr. Marshall. "We weren't sure exactly who or when. Walking through life can be beautiful; it can also be perilous. One must be attentive, always aware. Always."

We returned to our meditation while the body was silently removed and the blood wiped clean, leaving no trace of the sudden moment of violence. That killing was a profound lesson. Dr. Marshall was indeed a Shaolin master: a priest of priests, a warrior and a flower.

14

Insurgency: Counter Insurgency

DR. MARSHALL AND I quietly stood and exited his private refuge.

"You know," he said, "the pretense of nationalism has been a well-played fraud perpetrated on world citizens inherently given to adore their respective mother countries. The mass-mind propagandists have understood the phenomena of blind obedience for centuries: they play on a manufactured sense of loyalty, extracting allegiance and often the outright sacrifice of the lives of their ardent believers. Masterful and diabolical."

Dr. Marshall kept returning to this concept of mind manipulation: I would not call it a fixation, rather it was an over-arching realization to which his thoughts returned, time and again.

"Hitlerite, Goebbels correctly predicted that, if you tell a lie enough times, it will eventually be believed as truth.

They were masters of collective mind manipulation. This "art form" has just gotten better: with the advent of the Internet, the tools for mass mind influence has simply become more granular, more exact.

"It should be abundantly clear that this ball of mud and rock we call Earth is a closed system. The political, economic, and territorial boundaries are convenient illusions that permit the powerful to localize their control. It's fraud.

"Following the Second World War, the concept of a world government called the United Nations was a visionary concept designed to achieve a global sense of citizenship and interdependence. World citizenship versus pure nationalism.

"But the most powerful world players, led by the United States, were not interested in participating in a global forum. For them, the loss of dominance was and remains unthinkable. So, gradually and insidiously, support for a world-centric culture was starved to near death. What remains is an august body able to accomplish little. It is a symbolic reminder of possibilities. Symbols suggest reality but without substance: it's a farce. The UN also, regrettably, succumbed to greed and corruption. This must be purged.

"Better to point the finger at others than expose our own high crimes against humanity to the rule of international law. Distraction, delay, and denial are their time-honed tactics perfected to evade truth. Nice, huh?

"Ted Turnball and I each contributed one hundred billion dollars to the failing United Nations. This was born of an attempt to salvage one of the great concepts of modern times: a world with a single mind. But given the size of the problem, even two hundred billion is a pittance, falling far short of the real need. Aside from money, the will, the belief in the legitimacy of the concept, has been badly deflated.

"International courts were established to deal with crimes against humanity, yet we, notably, have refused to participate. Why?

"The crimes against humanity committed by our people are extensive and continuous. Yet in defiance of international convention, we wantonly torture, invade, and decimate countries and kill at will. Why would we want to subject ourselves to the jurisdiction of a world-established authority which would hold our politicians and military responsible for their actions? Instead of carrying the veil of integrity, we have become hated and despised. The eyes of the world are on us: We care not.

"Our prisons are crammed with the poor and largely colored peoples, while our schools are shut, classroom sizes increased, and the pay for teachers shrinks. What does THIS say about our priorities?

"The collective result is brazen and craven. We have fallen from grace.

"We have abandoned involvement. The biggest interest is in hegemony.

"This is the Mob in action. Kill and dominate without regret. Do whatever is necessary to advance the agenda of the few. Fuck the rest.

"Now the peak of the wave has arrived. Rex Donald's declaration of Martial Law and the suspension of all rights represents the culmination of a long-anticipated plan: global dominion. The absolute rule of the Mobsters, the oligarchs and the military. They are a cabal.

"Fortunately, there are enough of us spread throughout the world who are ferociously opposed to allowing this folly. As you will see, a multi-continental counterforce has been built to respond to this assault on human freedom. We may not win, but we fight fascism because it IS fascism.

"Failure to win will mean universal enslavement, poverty, and devastation. When Rex Donald hired you to eliminate me, he did not realize that I am but one of many — a snake with many heads poised to strike down the dark forces that have risen to the pinnacles of power. So even if you were successful in your mission, Santiago, the imperative for right would not die with me. Your effort would have been in vain."

Running down the long corridor came three massive dogs. They were beautiful — one fawn colored, another brindle, another gray.

"My babies," said Dr. Marshall. "Hello, my babies — two-hundred-and-fifty-pound babies — Old English mastiffs: Ludwig, Hannibal and Maximus."

Dr. Marshall snapped his fingers. The dogs sat in unison, completely understanding, adoring their friend and master. Dr. Marshall reached into a pocket in his robes and handed them each a large green treat. "Greenies, they love Greenies. Lots of chlorophyll, good for their stomachs and breath, and there is some magic ingredient which absolutely sends them into ecstasy."

Dr. Marshall had revealed yet another side of himself: a loving, caring man. The pleasure he took in greeting those dogs was overwhelming, and the first time I had seen him in full smile.

"They go everywhere with me," he continued. "They sleep at my bedside, they await while I shower, and they sit quietly while I eat, knowing that they are sure to get a bite. Absolute love. Complete devotion. Santiago, these guys only look like dogs, but they are not. They are sentient beings, messengers from God. I adore them."

From that point on, those dogs stuck by Dr. Marshall's side. They were a part of him: he was a part of them.

"Now, let's get down to how we are dealing with our world-wide reset."

15

Command and Control

WE WALKED ANOTHER hundred yards or so and again entered the vast control center. About a thousand people were poised over computers, all wearing head sets and glancing at an enormous array of screens around the perimeter of the room.

"So, Freddy, what's happening?" Dr. Marshall said to one of them. Like the others, the man was dressed in beautiful fitted black leather jacket, matching leather pants, and crimson tunic. He was clearly in command of the operation. Requiring no badge or emblem to identify himself as a leader, he exuded deliberate and quiet authority.

"Well, sir, our world partners are in full motion, have been ever since the bomb exploded yesterday."

"What happened to Santa Fe?" Dr. Marshall asked, knowing that the answer was not one he wanted to hear.

"All gone, leveled, flattened to the ground. All dead. It is the end for the Santa Fe Trail. Nothing left, sir. Nothing but rubble."

"And the surrounding ancient Indian pueblos?"

"The same — gone!"

"That bastard will pay. I have yet to decide exactly how, but I think some prolonged suffering is in order. I will not give him a quick death. That would be too merciful. We shall see what punishment fits this crime of all crimes." He paused, and then his expression brightened. "So Freddy, what's in motion?"

Freddy motioned to Dr. Marshall to follow him to a round glass table in the center of the control room. It was surrounded by white leather armchairs with chrome bases. The table was supported by a spectacular gleaming chrome flower-shaped base. Elegant, simple, and beautiful. Embedded in the glass top were a series of large color HD monitors, each tilted at a slight angle facing each of the chairs.

"Sir," said Freddy, "let's start with the money. As you know, we have set up an alternate system to the SWIFT international monetary transfer system. Trillions of dollars which were destined for the Caymans, Zurich, Luxembourg, Cyprus, Panama, and others have all been highjacked by our systems. The trillions drained from the world's treasuries are now in our safekeeping, safely preserved in our new bank in Antarctica.

"The precious metals intended to be stolen by Rex Donald, Molinov and the nouveau *capo de capos*, Gentile, have been seized by our forces. They were headed to storage bins in the Ural Mountains of Russia. We have them all. One hundred thousand of their guards were eliminated in the process. The funds are now in transit to Denmark, as we had planned."

"Good Freddy. Very good. What about the stock exchanges?"

"Sir, all have been shut. All the traders and "barons" have been shackled by our teams, worldwide. They are being led to various ships harbored around the globe and set to transport them all to our detention center in Tasmania. We have accommodations for about two hundred thousand of them.

"The oligarchs will receive special, different treatment.

"As you know, Dr. Marshall, these people were surrounded by heavily armed guards. We have neutralized them all with the nerve gas developed at our facilities here in New Mexico. They will awaken — perhaps a bit disoriented, but alive.

"The confrontation with their guards was carried out masterfully. Not a pretty sight, but treatment necessary given the gravity of the game now in play."

"Excellent, Freddy," nodded Dr. Marshall. "The militaries?"

"Not quite as clean as we had hoped. Every base around the United States and Russia has been attacked with neutron weapons. The facilities still stand, for the most part, but over five million of their military personnel have been evaporated. That's the beauty and terror of neutron weapons — but of course you know that. You and Dr. Cohen developed them. We had no choice."

"Unfortunate, but the removal of military force was mandatory," replied Dr. Marshall. "Without the power to respond, Rex Donald, Molinov, and Gentile are nothing more than paper tigers. Easier to cage."

"Yes, sir. No money, no force, no power.

"Freddy, you da man!" smiled Dr. Marshall.

"No nukes were fired," continued Freddy, "although it almost happened. From Russia aimed at the United States, and the United States set to deploy ICBMs towards Russia. We stopped that through electromagnetic shock waves sent around the globe from our network of satellites. Just in time, thank God, just in time."

"What about Washington and Moscow?"

"The power grids and transportation systems were instantly shut down. All telecommunications and Internet systems disabled. No one could communicate within or without. We deployed millions of men to each major city in Russia and the United States, with at least a million to Washington alone.

"Every government official of consequence has been seized, subdued, and is in transit to our Canadian holding camps.

"We do have a problem, however, with Rex Donald and Molinov: They have escaped. We are tracking them down. Our agents are very good, loyal and understand the significance attached to their capture. We will get them."

"I had hoped that we would have bagged them," said Dr. Marshall. "They are very resourceful and may have hidden assets and counter forces. We need to proceed, vigorously, in solving that problem. Gentile?"

"Jumped a private jet from Dulles to Palermo," said Freddy. "We could not detect his plane, probably flying too low. We think he headed to a plastic surgeon in Sicily for identity modification. We will have to genetically profile him when we close in on a likely subject. Our Italian affiliates are swarming over the island. It's just a matter of time."

"Time, Freddy, is not on our side. What about the people? Food, water, money, shelter, medical treatment?"

"All taken care of, sir — three hundred and fifty million in the U.S. and about two hundred million in Russia. All under control. Hospitals open, cash machines operating, food supplies abundant, hotels and shelters all open and free of charge, just as you instructed. The Chinese and Indians have cooperated beautifully. We may have to deal with them later, but for the moment, they support the change of the world order. So does most of Europe and Scandinavia. No problem with the Aussies and New Zealand. They're good people. Africa is too busy surviving.

"The Arabs and the North Koreans are still a problem. But we have crippled their infrastructure, primarily through electromagnetic paralysis. They are in the game for money: power, for them, is an afterthought.

"It worked just as you predicted.

"The world stockpile of energy," continued Freddy, "is intact and abundant. No one will go without. The Arab oil supplies have been seized and their leaders are all under house arrest.

"Kim in North Korea remains in hiding. That sick fuck is a problem. A big one."

"Russia and America," said Dr. Marshall, "are illusions convenient to the agendas of the oligarchs: countries kept in place long enough to serve them, but now abandoned as they always had intended. Their ethics and sense of social responsibility never really existed. It was a show, a sham." He turned to me. "Santiago, this mess is what you got suckered into. Proud?'

I said nothing.

"Freddy, something's not right," said Dr. Marshall. "I feel it. This has all gone too smoothly. Rex Donald and Molinov, I know them. They had to be anticipating that when they set their plans in motion there would be a strong counter-insurgency. These are not types to be caught surprised or unprepared. And Gentile is a vile, veteran mobster. A cockroach. This is a species that has survived for millions of years. They retreat into hidden places, mutate and return. We cannot permit him to survive. Their quiet retreat has got to be a show staged to distract. What do our colleagues around the world have to say? Ask them. Tell them I want to know what they think. Please, do it now!"

Freddy ran to his computer station, typed in a few sentences. Dr. Marshall was both brilliant and immaculately intuitive. My respect for Dr. Marshall —killer of my family, my jailer — had grown to become my teacher. I had turned a corner in my world: this Shaolin priest, astrophysicist, electronic tycoon, multi-billionaire, warrior, and ambassador had opened new doors in my perception. For the first time in my poisoned life, I could see a bright light shining. It was stunning and beautiful. I was drawn to its hypnotic glow. Where there had been a void in my being, suddenly that abyss had filled with unfathomable excitement and comfort.

"Freddy, we're going to have to dig into this ourselves," said Dr. Marshall. "As long as the head is alive, these putrid mutants can grow new bodies. We need their heads, literally and figuratively. We can't leave anything to chance."

Dr. Marshall turned to me. "Santiago, I know your mind. I infer no obligation and require nothing from you. I do, however, offer you a pathway to the light. This must be a road you are unhesitatingly willing to travel. Calming the mind is the ultimate challenge in any life. Stilling the noise within is akin to taming a rampaging elephant running wild in our thoughts. The reward is inner peace and access to your highest abilities and thoughts.

"I can see, behind your eyes, that you have seen the wonders of a clear course, a way out of the morass of the wrong. Are you game?"

I thought for several seconds: "You know I am, Dr. Marshall. I am, God help me, I am."

Dr. Marshall motioned to one of his aides. "We had these vestments prepared for you during the night. Changing your clothes will help you to change your mind.

An aide brought a beautiful crimson colored leather satchel. It was laid ceremoniously on the table. Dr. Marshall gently slid it in my direction.

"Now you are with us," he said. "Now you are one of us. All is forgiven: there is no past, only now and, perhaps, tomorrow. Why don't you step into the antechamber," to which he pointed. "You won't need your old garments: they are your history, while these are your tomorrow."

The butter-soft black leather jacket and pants, saffron colored undergarments, and a crimson short-collared silk turtleneck were perfectly packed into that precious case, as were perfectly polished black boots. Having dressed, I stepped back into the room. Dr. Marshall looked at me, warmly grinning.

"Good, very good. How do you feel?"

"Born again. Thank you, Doctor."

"Freddy, Call the airport. We need to get to Palermo. Let's start with one head of the snake."

Freddy returned to his station. Dr. Marshall's suspicions had been confirmed. Freddy explained that the "boys" had indeed survived. Alternate plans had been secretly made and armies amassed, hidden in mountains, caves, and undersea grottoes.

More importantly, Freddy exclaimed, they had developed an entirely new approach for weaponry: mass deployment of a genetic re-programing technology. Poised to be deployed throughout metropolitan water supply systems and remotely triggered, able to taint the drinking supply of major water systems worldwide.

Our enemies had their hands on a fundamental switch of life: DNA attenuation. They held the key to altering not only the physical nature of the world — they could also change the consciousness of the collective mind. This held the potential for societal extortion — cultural blackmail, the key to human subjugation.

"This is an ultimate power," Dr. Marshall spoke as he closed his eyes, seemingly searching into space for actionable answers.

16

World Without Borders

WE STOOD, ALL understanding the significance of what lay before us. All at the conference table followed Dr. Marshall, robes flowing, to the major portal of the control center. Dr. Marshall turned to his staff: the eyes of a thousand men and women lovingly fixed on him. He turned and raised his hands in a demonstration of deep respect and compassion.

He spoke in his bass baritone voice that carried unimpeded through that vast room: "Peace and love to you all. All will be well. May light continue to shine on your gentle souls. From the bottom of my heart, I thank you all. The world thanks you all."

Dr. Marshall slowly lowered his hands, his eyes mysteriously locked with all who were gathered before him. His benevolence was profound.

We exited the main chamber and stepped into the station where our vacuum transport vehicle, doors opened, awaited.

"Santiago, please sit with me," said Dr. Marshall. "Our airfield is one hundred miles away, but at four hundred miles per hour our hop will take less than fifteen minutes. I want to begin our new connection with a simple but important teaching. Perhaps you will like it. Each teaching has the potential to open permanent doors in your mind. Once unsealed, you can never forget. That's the beauty of a ringing bell: once rung, impossible to un-ring."

The capsule, like everything in Dr. Marshall's private world, was simple and immaculate. One fresh red rose in a simple crystal bud vase sat on a white marble table between us. Dr. Marshall and I sat facing each other. Our other associates took their seats, which were placed in precise alignment down the corridors of the cabin.

"I would like you to understand that we are facing the essence of evil on earth," Dr. Marshall said to me. "Perhaps such evil has always existed. What makes this current manifestation so deadly is the mastery we human beings have gained over the physical universe. Einstein, through theoretical thought alone, envisioned the equivalence of energy and matter. That thought experiment, later confirmed by demonstrable physics, changed the world.

"Buddha was also a kind of theoretical physicist: a spiritual physicist. Most think that Buddhist thought is a religion. It is not.

"It is a philosophy: an understanding about the forces of nature, of the vectors of life which flow through us all. Buddha realized that, without compassion, greed and anger would rule men forever.

"He realized the absolute need to transcend that trap. But how? Where should one look for the answers to the ancient riddle which has doomed men and women to repeat history, time and again? Hard-fought historic victories all eventually disappear and leave us to repeat insanity — maybe dancing to different music, but still trapped by an eternal theme of moral squalor.

"Buddha Shakyamuni was a man, not a God. He never proclaimed to be, and anyone who knows about his life or real teachings would agree. He as a man born of extraordinary privilege — a prince, in fact.

"His father protected his young and beautiful son from seeing the deprivation that lay just outside the walls of his gilded palace. Like any loving parent, he wanted to shield his son from experiencing the surrounding suffering. His father had the means to do that, and for years succeeded in distracting his son, enveloping him with riches and beauty.

"Was this a gift or a curse?

"There came a time when the secrets of suffering could no longer be hidden from the young man. He ventured out and what he saw changed his life and the lives of billions to come.

"Buddha saw pain, poverty, suffering, and death. He had never known these before. He was dumbstruck with how limited his own perceptions of the world had been. He could not abide or reconcile his advantage knowing the utter misery of others.

"To make a very long story — and over fifty thousand spoken lessons — short, the world inherited the wisdom which sprung from this remarkable being.

"When I realized that I too had come from an advantaged world — a corrupt one — I could relate, in my own small way, to the enormity of that man's mind and the lessons he derived from his realizations born of true compassion and empathy. He was no better or worse than others. The advantages of his birth did not entitle him to anything, since, as flesh, he too would succumb to the unstoppable forces of nature. All things corrupt and die. They rust into nothingness. They disappear into time."

Dr. Marshall closed his eyes, knowing that he had just encapsulated for me the realization that had taken him a lifetime to comprehend. He did it in just a few simple, elegant sentences. The clarity of his words was dazing and penetrating.

"I am not a saint, martyr or idealist," he continued. "I am, despite the trappings of a life well-lived, quite simple in what I have come to value as important.

"Rex Donald and his kind represent a fundamental depravity I have never been able to countenance. There lies within such people a terrible condescension, an imagined entitlement, which says, 'I am worth everything; you are worth nothing! My life is important; yours it not. My *wants* are my *needs*.'

"Santiago, this kind of thinking is premised on a disgusting sense of superiority. It runs counter to the intention of nature. I hated it even before I understood why.

"One sees many depictions and poses of Buddha. They are not different depictions of deities, they are symbolic representations of the different intentions of Buddha. Remember this: There is only one depiction of perfection. It may be reflected in different faces, but those faces, unmasked, are the same face, the kind face of a simple man who I have come to respect and love — a man long gone in a physical sense, but in a spiritual context, here with us, now and forever.

"Was Jesus or Moses or Muhammad among those enlightened? Perhaps. But the one with whom I have been able to most closely identify is the gifted being from the mountains of Asia.

"Like him, I ask you to believe nothing. To accept nothing. To buy nothing. Take only what rings true to you and leave the rest. This is the simple beauty of it all. Exquisite."

We had arrived at the airfield terminal. The ride had been without vibration or any sense of acceleration — extraordinary!

"OK, let's get this show on the road," Dr. Marshall said casually, as if it were a matter of fact.

We stepped off an elevator onto the tarmac of Dr. Marshall's private jetport. An amazing aircraft stood gleaming in the desert sun. With an enormous wingspan, it was at least the size of two football fields in length. In a very strange geometry, four very large engines hung from its wings, which were covered in a kind of black ceramic array. "

"I've never seen a plane like this before," I said to Dr. Marshall. "What is it?"

"It's my hypersonic solar-powered jet. We developed the technology at our labs not far from here. This craft can achieve Mach four — that's four times the speed of sound or nearly three thousand miles-per-hour. We'll be in Palermo in two hours.

"We finally figured out how to create a propulsion system thousands of times more powerful than the most advanced standard technologies. We use a laser bombardment technique which vastly increases the surface area of the solar generating cells, so for the same geometry, we're able to achieve exponentially more power. We call it black sand. Very cool!

Dr. Marshall's surprises seemed to be limitless.

"Let's board," he said. "For the first time in his ignoble life, Mr. Luigi Gentile needs to be brought to heel."

With a full-fledged communications and control center, the cabin of the aircraft was designed both for seating and action. "All of our facilities, around the world, are interconnected in real time," said Dr. Marshall as we settled into soft leather seats. "We're all reading from the same page, second by second. We need one collective mind with which we can focus our determination.

"I want you to know that I am not doing this for myself. This really has nothing to do with me. We are dealing with the interests of humankind. I am a means to an end, not the end."

The doors of the cabin were closed by armed attendants.

"One other thing as we get going, Santiago," said Dr. Marshall. "Evil is not something outside of us. While we can point to obvious dark spots and beings in the world around us, it's harder for us to point to these spots within ourselves. We implicitly give credence to our own dark forces by denying their existence, or worse still, by admiring them.

"Envy of the wealthy and powerful is endemic in the United States. We have a nefarious history of worshiping those who have, through whatever reason, risen to the top of the social heap. This kind of admiration is actually a sickness. It imbues credence to those who *have* and implicitly denigrates those who *have not*.

"Thugs like Rex Donald exist, in part, because we admire them. We want to be like them. At the end of the day, despite his wealth and influence, Luigi Gentile is nothing but a punk. Like a movie star, we bestow credibility in those who have achieved notoriety; in his case, the notoriety is couched in cruelty and heartlessness. Beings like this exist because of our inherent inability and reluctance to recognize bad in others.

"So, even though I detest our band of 'bad boys,' I also detest that residual tendency which dwells within us to pay tribute to those who deserve none. I include myself in this self-indictment. Hopefully, at this juncture in my life, I have stepped beyond."

17

Aloft

FLYING HYPERSONICALLY IS a thrilling notion, even though, after the initial experience of G force acceleration, the sense of speed is imperceptible. Watching the airspeed meter and how rapidly we were traversing the United States and then out over the open Atlantic was exhilarating.

We were headed to the airport in Palermo, Sicily — the only field in the area with a runway long enough to accommodate our aircraft. Dr. Marshall was in close consultation with several of his associates, dancing from seat to seat, table to table, bent over in deep discussions. This was serious business and the magnitude of the impending outcome was unmistakable.

"Santiago," he said to me, "I think we've found a way to defuse one of their most onerous threats: the DNA reprogramming and water supply poisoning. Our scientists at Kirtland Air Force Base in Albuquerque — the Sandia Lab guys — have come up with a way of simultaneously disarming the mechanisms planted in each of the reservoirs. Ultrasonic contra-sound beamed from our network of satellites is likely to do the trick. The devices planted by Rex and his henchmen are hardwired to resist radio wave interference. They correctly anticipated that vulnerability, but ultra-sonic counter radiation is not a spectrum they had anticipated. Enter stage left!"

Dr. Marshall was given to a funny kind of hyperbole: "Enter stage left! Let's get the show on the road! Cool!" These were unlikely words coming from him; but, after all, he was a child of the sixties. Once exposed to the San Francisco of those Grateful Dead days, one can never forget — and why would you want to anyway? Dr. Marshall continued to fascinate me with his range of emotions and language. Very curious.

"In about fifteen seconds," he continued, "we will attempt to neutralize their nasty little boxes and remotely test whether our efforts worked. I have an eighty-five-percent confidence level." Spoken like the true scientist he was: no absolutes, just probabilities and statistical windows. Another point of fascination from his endless stream of surprises.

Freddy approached, smiling: "Voilà, Doctor — it worked!"

Openly pleased, Dr. Marshall grinned with intense relief. Had President Donald's devilish ploy worked, the entire game could have changed. Paint another angel on our fuselage.

"Now Freddy," said Dr. Marshall, "if Rex and Molinov are playing with DNA, they must have some very heavy people working on it. We can't underestimate their abilities. When we find Gentile, who is probably under the knife of plastic surgeons as we speak, there is a chance they may have been able to alter his genetic fingerprint. We've got to anticipate that.

"Do we have any retinal scans of Gentile? Check our databases — perhaps we have a hacked scan from some retinal identification system in an airport or a secure facility. That prick has free access to everything!"

Freddy went back to his console and returned a moment later. "Yes sir, right here," he said as he held up two high-resolution films labeled as the vascular retinal signatures of Luigi Gentile.

"Excellent," said Dr. Marshall, "but we need to think past this. If they have the ability to falsify DNA signatures, they may be able to reconfigure even delicate retinal arterial patterns. Let's think about it, OK?"

Several minutes further into our flight, now probably mid-Atlantic, all the window shades of the plane suddenly closed and the jet took a steep dive before swerving left and right.

"We're under attack," Dr. Marshall said calmly.

Several passengers were thrown violently about the cabin. Those who were standing managed to regain their seats and secure their restraining harnesses, bloodied and shocked.

"Dr. Marshall," a voice over the voice system announced in impeccable British English, "We have incoming from satellite-launched missiles. In response we're deploying counter measures and decoys. Meanwhile, please remain in your seats with your safety harnesses fastened."

"My pilot," smiled Dr. Marshall. "Former Royal Air Force. Nerves of steel."

To me, the pilot words were nice, but under the circumstances not terribly comforting.

"I expected this possibility," continued Dr. Marshall. "With luck we'll dodge the assault. Hang on!" Dr. Marshall was cool, even in starring down imminent death.

He had told me, in one of our peripatetic conversations, that the Buddhists believed that the state of one's mind, exactly at the moment of death, was a crucial determinant of the kind of afterlife one would experience. Entering the realm of rebirth was directly related, he said, to one's intentions, level of happiness, and peace at the precise moment of death. Therefore, since the end could come for all of us, without notice, it was vital to maintain an even mental keel and a very high level of tranquility at all times. The door to forever can open anytime, anywhere. The penalty for not maintaining a peaceful mind could involve being condemned to repeated earthly lifetimes — for most souls, consuming all of time. Dr. Marshall believed this, and I was beginning to believe it as well. In any event, who wants to play with that?

After several minutes of wild aerial twisting, the plane leveled out. We had escaped extinction.

"What's clear here, Santiago, is that our 'friends' are well-prepared," said Dr. Marshall as he unbuckled his safety harness. "We may have dismantled their known infrastructure, military, and finances, but there is obviously much we have not anticipated. A potentially lethal omission!"

We touched down, feather light, at Palermo airport. As we pulled to a stop, I saw hundreds of large camouflaged helicopters idling on the huge field, their rotors spinning lazily under the brilliant blue sky. Sicily is a fortress land mass which has long stood defiant against the surrounding Ionian and Mediterranean Seas. The island is within a lick of the coast of the African continent, an historically important access point in trade and military routes which connected Asia, Africa, and Europe. Like its people, it endures, forever rugged and rebellious.

Dr. Marshall led the way off the plane. On the tarmac, several men dressed in black and crimson approached him. No detail was accidental for Dr. Marshall. He appreciated symmetry. For him, I was growing to appreciate that aesthetics and function were interwoven concepts. Really quite lovely.

After speaking with the men, Dr. Marshall turned to me. "We're going to Syracuse, to the Gentile villas. Our associates have been informed that Luigi Gentile has built his own hospital on the grounds of his forefathers. This would be the most likely place to find him. The Italians nest close to their historical roots, to their families. Life may be complex, but for them, some things are sacrosanct, and a home that can be defended provides the safest and most comforting of all harbors. It's an ancient instinct, and with good reason."

We boarded the choppers, and with a collective roar all soared aloft in unison. Turning southeast, we headed to Syracuse, the ancient Roman city poised on the azure Ionian Sea. This is where the Gentiles had, for generations, maintained their thousands of acres of vineyards and monumental villas.

The choppers, escorted by a squadron of Harrier jets, closed in on the Gentile estates, vast and magnificent.

As we approached the grounds of the largest and most opulent estate, our airborne convoy was attacked with missiles, ground fire, and flack: a full assault. But despite their considerable fortifications and aggression, the Gentile forces were no match for those of Dr. Marshall. Within minutes all was quiet: neutralized.

The view from above the Gentile compound was impressive: a complex of ancient villas nestled in luscious gardens, ringed by flowering lemon trees. The grounds were groomed, with every branch, every plant lovingly and exactly placed. The elegance of the Italians is without parallel.

We set down our chopper near an ancient fountain of Poseidon. The other choppers in our squad spread out and set down wherever enough open space was available.

We entered what appeared to be the main villa, magnificent and regal, yet welcoming. The entry way supported a cupola that must have been four stories high, while a stained glass ceiling depicted a breathtaking mural that looked like a work of Michelangelo.

So, this was the home of perhaps the wealthiest man on earth. No mobster trappings were anywhere in sight — just sheer class.

At the top of a double spiral staircase stood one of the most beautiful women I had ever imagined. Her long black hair draped over her ample breasts. Her lips were like rose petals, and she wore a simple rose-colored ancient Roman-style stola. Her head was adorned with a golden tiara — perfect elegance.

"May I help you gentlemen?" she asked in a honeyed voice.

Dr. Marshall replied, "We are here to see Signore Gentile."

"Oh, I must apologize; he is away — I think on business." It was a beautiful lie told by a beautiful woman. We were not convinced, but it was hard not to be enchanted by her hypnotic countenance and her seductive voice.

"With respect, signora, we believe he is here," Freddy said.

"Perhaps you gentlemen would enjoy some refreshments. I will have some of our finest wines and fruits from our vineyards prepared; we can share in the gardens."

"Your offer is most gracious, signora, but we are here on serious business." Dr. Marshall was deferential to Signora Gentile, but resolutely firm. "Perhaps we can avail ourselves of your considerable hospitality at another time."

"Very well. I cannot help you. My husband is not on our estates. Perhaps you should return."

"Perhaps not, signora. We have every reason to believe he is here. Please spare my troops from having to search through your properties; but we will if you continue to refuse." Dr. Marshall was not buying any of it!

Signora Gentile was carrying out the role she was born to perform: the protection of her family. This is universal, but an especially Italian virtue.

Several hundred of our associates set out in all directions, and the search for Luigi Gentile was on. The estate was very large and we knew the hunt might take hours.

Dr. Marshall and I rested in chairs surrounding an enchanting fountain under the cupola. The pungent smell of lemon flowers perfumed the air. This hardly seemed like the home of a brazen killer — the *capo de capos*.

"We think we've found him," reported a soldier, "or someone who might be him. Please, sir, follow us."

Entering a wrought iron cage elevator, we descended several stories. The elevator opened onto a large, bright white space — a hospital that had been constructed underground, ultra-modern and very well-equipped. Doctors and nurses were scurrying, carrying charts, pushing carts.

"Where is he?" Dr. Marshall was not impressed by any of this. Though charming, Dr. Marshall had a no-nonsense side to him. Tough. Formidable.

We were led through a series of corridors to a room. A man with a bandaged face lay in a hospital bed surrounded by an array of medical equipment, intravenous pumps, electronic monitors. He wanted for nothing.

"Take a sample of his saliva, please, Freddy." Dr. Marshall knew that time was working against us: we needed to get on with our mission. Freddy took out a box containing a hand-held device and some cotton swabs on long sticks. He donned surgical gloves, approached the bed, and inserted the cotton tipped probe in the mouth of the patient.

"Test it, Freddy."

Responding immediately to Dr. Marshall's directive, Freddy inserted the swab into a portal in the hand-held DNA analyzer. The computer in the device quickly analyzed the sample.

"Dr. Marshall, this is not Luigi Gentile. The match is good, but not perfect; and it must be."

Dr. Marshall had anticipated this. "Let me see it." He read the complex patterns on the display screen of the device. This device, he said, was originally developed by one of the U.S. National Labs to identify remains of fallen soldiers in Viet Nam. He was one of the young scientists who had helped to perfect the technology — another Dr. Marshall surprise.

"Yes, you're right," he announced. "The sequences are close but not exact." How did they do this? The genetic alternation of some cells seemed possible — but not all.

"Roll him over and stick a probe up his ass." Assisted by three men, Freddy did as requested.

The nurses and doctors in attendance were obviously nervous and spoke rapidly in animated Italian. I could not judge if they were concerned for themselves or their patient.

The new sample was processed and again the profile did not match Gentile's.

"Let's try the retinal scan."

"Yes, sir." Freddy reached into a small pouch and removed a silver ophthalmic scanner, which he placed over one of the open eyes of the patient. After pressing a small red button, he read the display.

"I'm sorry, Dr. Marshall. Again, the scan is close but not a match."

"They altered the patterns of the arterial retinal array," replied Dr. Marshall. "Very clever. Only one surgeon in the world could do this. He must be here. His name is Dr. Melvin Betram from New York Eye and Ear Hospital. He won a Nobel Prize for perfecting a surgical technique for retinal re-attachment of over-oxygenated premature infants. Really quite brilliant. I know him from our Harvard Mass General days when I was studying biophysics. I want you to find him!"

"Yes, sir."

Fifteen minutes later, a rotund, jolly looking mustachioed doctor dressed in surgical scrubs appeared.

"Hello Bertie, you piece of shit," said Dr. Marshall.

"Nice to see you too, James!"

"I wish I could reciprocate. Tell me what you did to this man. Retinal array modification?"

"He's my patient, James, you know I can't tell you."

"Don't fuck with me Bertie! Nobel Prize or not, you are expendable!"

"I can't. I won't."

Dr. Marshall turned to Freddy. "I am not going to allow this maggot to jeopardize our mission. Let's make some plant fertilizer." He then addressed Dr. Betram: "You're a stupid bastard throwing your life away for a mobster. I always knew you were an afflicted moron! Go fuck yourself."

Freddy quickly produced a small weapon from his jacket pocket. It looked like a laser gun. He held it to Dr. Bertram's head and pulled the trigger. Before Dr. Bertram had time to react, he was reduced to a small pile of dust on the floor. Dr. Bertram was burnt toast.

"Sprinkle him in the garden," commanded Dr. Marshall. "Better yet, flush him down the toilet with your next crap. When my son died and I asked for his help in managing the forensic investigation, he told me that my son was better off dead. Ciao, Bertie!"

With determination in his voice, Dr. Marshall then commanded, "Continue the search! The poor bastard in this hospital bed is a sham, a shill. Gentile is here, somewhere."

One of Dr. Marshall's associates, a lovely woman, approached and spoke with excitement and animation. "Dr. Marshall, we found another wing! Maybe we've found Luigi Gentile posing as another so-called patient!"

"Let's see."

As we turned to leave the room, Signora Gentile stood in the doorway. She seemed to have materialized from nowhere.

"Ah, signora, *bon journo*." Dr. Marshall had flawless manners. He obviously liked women, and especially beautiful women.

"I would like to accompany you."

"Not a problem; you might be helpful." Dr. Marshall was deliberate in his every word and deed.

We followed our new female associate down a maze of hospital corridors and arrived at a room with double doors: an operating room.

Doctors and nurses were standing over their male patient, applying final bandages to his face. His fingers were already surgically dressed: fingerprints obviously changed, probably with acids or lasers.

"Freddy, you know the drill," said Dr. Marshall.

The DNA swab of the epithelial cells in the mouth was obtained and the results examined. Still not a match—close, but not perfect.

"Now his ass, Freddy—let's check down there." Again, not a match. How had the Gentile gang accomplished this? Was this yet another decoy?

"Retinas, please, Freddy." Again a scan: close but not confirmatory.

"Fuck, fuck! We've got to be sure," said Dr. Marshall.

The patient had been intubated and was dependent on a breathing machine. Facial transplant is a long and complex procedure requiring deep anesthesia. He was just coming up from the anesthetics, but his breathing was labored. He was, I think, hooked to that machine because the operation did not go as planned. There had been complications.

"Signora Gentile, come over here," ordered Dr. Marshall. "Stand next to me."

Both Dr. Marshall and Signora Gentile stood next to the now groggy but awakened patient. Looking up from between slits in the bandages, his eyes locked with Signora Gentile's.

His eyes teared. It was him: the *capo de capos*, perhaps the most powerful man on earth, laid out, helpless.

"Signora, perhaps it's time for you to leave." Dr. Marshall spoke to her gently and with utter politesse.

"That will not be necessary, Doctor Marshall," she replied. Without hesitation she walked over to the respirator, located the power switch, and turned it off. It was done.

"I have lived the life of a golden bird in a barbed-wire cage," she said. "I have had everything, yet I have had nothing. This monster attempted to hide, to dodge my questions — but I knew. We all knew. Bury his carcass behind the pig pen. Suitable, don't you think, Dr. Marshall?"

18

Moscow

"THIS IS NOT going to be easy, Dr. Marshall," I said. "Molinov must have enormous defenses, even though we've destroyed those already known to us."

Dr. Marshall turned to me with a Cheshire grin. A master on top of his game is something to behold.

"I've already arranged for exactly the help we need, from those who hate Russia most: Chechnya and Afghanistan. The Russians have brutalized their populations for decades. In the case of Afghanistan, they are unconquerable. For the Chechens, brutal decimation. These people *never* forget. Now we will provide them with opportunity to remember."

"If we launched a frontal assault to get Molinov, we would meet with fierce and terrible resistance. Better go through the back door, here.

"For decades the Russians attempted to overwhelm and capture Afghanistan. The war broke their bank and the will of their people. Even a severely oppressed public will eventually rise up and say, enough! When enough of their sons and daughters come home in body bags, the appetite for conquest fades. In addition, the decades-long attempt by the Russians to have Afghanistan broke the Kremlin's bank. They could not continue to fight the Cold War with the rest of the world, control their conquered Iron Curtain territories, and wage a bitter conflict in the mountains of Asia.

"So, being the idiots we are, the U.S. took over where the Russians left off: jumping on a train bound for nowhere. Our adventure in Afghanistan will cost enormous treasure and lives, wasted for nothing. Yet another example of history senselessly repeating itself. There is an awful flaw in us humans. I wish I could wave a wand and fix it all. Instead, I'm left to pick off smaller pieces. We do what we can, Santiago."

Dr. Marshall had arranged with the Chechens and the Afghans to do what they do best: terrorize. The arch-enemies of Russia had infiltrated many parts of Russia. We had suspected that Molinov was in hiding in the mountains close to Kazakhstan — ironically, quite close to the uranium mines owned by the Marshall family. Dr. Marshall's intelligence was, again, spot on.

Molinov had set up an extensive operations center in the mine tunnels of Kazakhstan. Aided by the use of bunker busting bombs and nerve agents, several hundred thousand troops infiltrated the tunnels, finally locating the bombastic Molinov.

Molinov had attempted to set off a nuclear confrontation from the ground, air, and sea. Orbiting space platforms were also set to deploy warheads. Dr. Marshall had correctly predicted this and neutralized Molinov with the use of enough powerful electromagnetic radiation to cripple the Russian command and control centers, their computers, and weapons.

Molinov, realizing that there was no escape, surrendered himself to the Chechen invaders, who were under strict instructions from Dr. Marshall not to rip him to pieces. I am told that their temptation to do just that was nearly overwhelming.

Dr. Marshall had made sure that Molinov, another nuclear freak, would be treated carefully. Dr. Marshall had other plans for Molinov: a rendezvous with his colleague, President Rex Donald. They deserved each other. Dr. Marshall was going to see to it that they would spend an appropriate amount of time together: forever.

19

Amerika

"AMERIKA: LAND OF illusion and broken dreams. Land of freedom and hope. Land of great intentions and horrific atrocities. Land of immigrants and opportunity. Land of poverty and illiteracy.

"Did you know, Santiago, that in comparison to a country like Denmark, the poverty rate in Amerika is nearly twenty percent of the population? Over ten percent of our population has no health insurance, while in Denmark everyone is covered. Guaranteed vacation time in the U.S. is zero, while in Denmark it's five weeks. In the United States, people work about eighteen hundred hours per year, and in Denmark, fourteen hundred. Government revenues as a percent of GDP in the U.S. are thirty-three percent, and in Denmark fifty-six percent! Add to this that a good percentage of the money collected in the U.S. from taxes is actually used to service interest payments for multi-trillion-dollar debt, so even though the U.S. taxes its people every day and in every way, relatively little gets to the *people*.

"China, Russia, Saudi Arabia, India, France, United Kingdom, Japan, and Germany spend together less for their armed forces, *combined*, than the United States, which tops the world charts at over six hundred billion dollars yearly, and that's just the money in the budget! We spend billions more on "black research," known only to those who need to know.

"So while we stand ready to destroy the planet, our people are illiterate, taxed, and worked to death, and sold a bill of goods that everything is just fine!"

As usual, Dr. Marshall knew the numbers on the planetary scoreboard. His point was clear: We have been told that we are the richest, most wonderful place on earth, and yet, we are clearly *not*.

"Great PR, right Santiago? How much longer do you think the public is going to swallow this kind of bitter pill? Where would you place your bet?

"There's more, and it's much worse than these miserable statistics. These numbers belie a fundamental disgusting elitism. As I have previously attempted to explain, this goes back to our great but often ignominious roots. The history lessons I was taught in my high school years conveniently skipped over much of the truth. No use tainting tender young minds of the postwar boomers: the world was freed, for a time, from the tyranny of dictatorial maniacs and placed in the loving hands of powerful corporations now beginning their insidious move towards global domination and military insanity, and the concomitant degradation of the very people who had vested vast power in governmental bodies. We were taught that this would be a fair exchange. I think we now understand how that turned out!

"Let's jump back to Alamogordo and what ensued. As my father correctly understood, once unleashed, everyone wanted the power to destroy. The result is that the world has been in constant conflict since the end of the Second World War, and the planet is armed to the teeth. Despite numerous attempts to reduce the global arsenal, thousands of strategic and nuclear weapons are poised for delivery from land, aircraft, sea, and now, space.

"The planet yearns for wisdom and leaders who can halt what has got to be a certain showdown with what will be the complete destruction of civilization.

"Although global nuclear stockpiles have been reduced from their previous level of being able to destroy the earth fifty times over, mankind still has the power to vaporize the planet in excess of merely ten times! First you kill, then you kill then again, then again and again and again and again. Got it, Santiago? That's what we're dealing with.

"Sure, rogue weapons have fallen into the hands of terrorist actors; but at the center of this global black heart of hell sit the tyrants who inhabit the granite halls of the world's major capitols. Washington, D.C., is at the epicenter of the action.

"Now that Rex Donald is president, the danger of a global holocaust is ever present. I am tempted to publish the audiotapes I have of his proclamations spoken to me so many years ago. The public should know exactly who has seized the reins of power.

"Ironically, even if we stop him, we will not stop the global recklessness which has befallen the people of the world; but we will have significantly decreased the odds and, hopefully, in the process, refocused our attention on building a global consciousness of compassion and human responsibility — a responsibility we have an implicit obligation to fulfill.

"This is the ultimate roll of the dice, Santiago. My entire life has brought me to this place. That I have been so close to the ones who were prime movers in this terrible drama of impending destruction is an irony that has consumed my consciousness.

"After my experience in protecting my family's Russian assets; after a failed, bitter marriage; and after squandering a large portion of my life with frivolity, my Buddhist teachings have completely re-centered my purpose."

Dr. Marshall proceeded to explain that he knew that President Rex Donald had been in the White House residence. He would have greatly preferred returning to New York, but New York City is one of the most populated places on earth. Defending Rex Donald, even with his private armies, would be difficult in New York. So, reluctantly the president had remained in Washington, stripped of the military, which had either been neutralized by Dr. Marshall or had defected.

Getting to the president, Dr. Marshall explained, could be accomplished surgically by just one person.

"Do you know who that person is, Santiago?" he said with a smile. He didn't have to tell me the answer.

Oh joy! But Rex Donald owed me, and I intended to collect. Doing so in person? OK, I could handle that, I thought.

Dr. Marshall had all of the details well planned. The master in motion, again.

20

Santa Fe?

"To die, to sleep – to sleep, perchance
to dream – ay, there's the rub."

Shakespeare, *Hamlet*

THE FLIGHT FROM Joint Base Andrews to Sante Fe was unremarkable. An Air Force Gulfstream jet had been placed at my disposal, ordered by President Rex Donald. We had just finished meeting in the residence at the White House. An off-calendar meeting: slipping in and slipping out.

The president had demanded my attendance. He made it clear that he was concerned about Dr. Marshall and wanted me to investigate. He handed me an electronic funds transfer confirmation: a deposit of ten million dollars in my Panamanian account had been completed about an hour before the meeting. Ten million, in the course of things, is not a fortune, especially when dealing with billionaires. For President Donald, this was donut money. For me, not a bad payday, especially for an initial explanatory trip.

The president had made it clear that this was a down payment. There would be more to follow, but more than a mere "investigation" should be expected. We both knew what he meant. I do not hire out to go grocery shopping.

I stretched out on a couch toward the rear of the jet and slept like a tuckered-out infant. Just another trip on another job. I had no sense that this was anything other than routine. I had not been to Santa Fe in years. I was always comfortable there and looked forward to the visit, despite the directive I had been assigned by President Rex Donald.

A short taxi ride to my favorite boutique hotel, The Anastasi in downtown Santa Fe, just off a lovely tree-lined plaza complete with Spanish-style gazebo. It was Christmas, with the ground snow packed with a thousand colored lights laced through the trees. Charming.

The bellboy escorted me to my room. I undressed quickly, carefully hanging my silver raw silk double-breasted suit in the chifferobe. I placed my white starched shirt, still relatively unwrinkled, and silver and black horizontally striped silk tie on a hanger next to my suit. My shoes, still perfectly shined, placed neatly on the floor of the closet. I had always been a stickler for physical symmetry and orderliness: it inferred to me a sense that all was right in the world.

I showered and dried. It was refreshing and the smell of mint soap and body wash was lovely. I pulled back the sheet, grabbing the edge to form a perfect triangle, exposing a slot for me to slide under the covers without ruffling the exquisitely made bed: satin sheets, pillow cases, the bed covered with a white, red, and orange wool Indian Pendleton blanket. The Southwest is a special place.

I dropped off the earth into a sleep of total relaxation. Gone.

Slits of sun came through the wooden shutters. These were Kodachrome dreams, transported through an extravagant voyage. The cavalcade of my dreams was unprecedented: stunning, dimensional, and played out with all my senses fully engrossed. Dr. Marshall, Santa Fe, Palermo, Moscow: all of it, a twist of mind, a fluke, hallucination?

A light knock at the door: on my feet now, I swung the terrycloth robe hanging in the bathroom suite over my shoulders and opened the hand-forged door to my hotel suite.

No one.

An envelope had been slipped under the threshold. It was a brilliant white sleeve of the finest stationery. How consistent with a first-class hotel: a personalized greeting note.

No, not from the hotel. The engraved inscription on the back of the envelope:

Marshall

I quickly opened the letter.

Dr. James Marshall
Sometime, Somewhere

My Dear Santiago:

We almost met! Funny, that!

I fully intended to bump into you at the emergency room at Santa Fe Hospital. That was your plan, no?

Some biological distractions interrupted my well-intentioned plans. By the time you read this, my soul will have left my body, bound for I know not where.

Read: Dead.

You will recall that I told you about my childhood in Alamogordo, and the radiation. Cancer linked to it that took my entire family. I survived, at least for a good long time. Finally caught up with me, metastasized throughout my body. No chance of recovery. So, on to the next chapter!

Don't worry, all we think is illusion: often times very convincing.

Some advice: Don't sweat the little stuff.

Barring meeting you in body, I decided to default to next best method: to meet you in your sleeping mind.

I trust you had a pleasant rest. Thanks for leaving the doors to your psyche so wide open. What a pleasure walking through. Quite a wild ride, wouldn't you say?

Santiago, the dreams I dreamed for you portend the future. It is not a question of whether those dreams could be real: they will! The play is already in motion: you know that.

My reality has become my dreams and my dreams have become my reality. I wish this gift for you.

You have been a very good student. I regret not having more time to show you what I have learned in my passage through this world. Perhaps we'll meet again.

In the meantime, you've seen the movie. Truth cannot be hidden from any state of mind.

Don't fret over the question of whether your dreams are imaginary or real. These are trivialities better left to lesser men.

Your dreams contain instructions. I think you know what has to be done.

My dear student, although I have been given much, I have always understood that much is expected from the blessed. I have welcomed and embrace this implied covenant.

Please know that I was born as a Baby Boomer, literally and figuratively. At the end of a massive global war and in the wake of the first atomic explosion.

I have considered myself as a Boomer intensively caring. As I write these final words to you, I am, my designated assassin and student, reaching my final moments in earthly coils, in intensive care.

Knowing you now dwell in the realm of light provides me with deep solace and a confirmation that there is hope. Where there is hope, there is life. Where there is life, there is love.

I consider myself fortunate in having survived this long. I regret nothing.

Carry the torch for as long as you can. More importantly, pray for those who will rise up against dystopia. They are our children, Santiago. We *all deserve to dwell in a wonderful universe. You understand.*

The cosmos will protect you. There is nothing to fear, come what may.

Happy Trails,
Dr. James Marshall

What magic had Dr. Marshall conjured? I had returned to Santa Fe. I thought I had been here before, and that I had walked through an epic journey with Dr. Marshall. Yet I was here, I think now, for the first time. The mind can play unfathomable tricks.

Tricks played by a man I had never actually met.

Stepping to the window of the Anastasi Hotel off that sweet plaza in downtown Santa Fe, all seemed quiet and tidy. The buildings stood, cars passed, people were settling down, bundled from the cold, headed for *al fresco* breakfast at the café across the street. Nothing had been leveled. There were no signs of destruction. Just an old western town poised for another day at the end of the Santa Fe Trail.

My dreams had painted a very different picture: a devastated town, thousands dead, a global confrontation, a galactic struggle between dark and light.

I had dreamed a dream. It was just a dream. None of it was real. The details of my fantasy ride were astonishing and fully dimensioned. Could this be? Is the mind capable of such sorcery?

Before me was a scene of tranquility and absolute normalcy. This was not a dream, or was it? Which is the dream; which is the real? Goddamn it, Dr. Marshall, you're fucking with me!

I laughed. Dr. Marshall was a master. He could do as he wished. Poor little me.

My cell phone chimed. Restricted number. I answered.

"Well, what's happening?" It was the president of the United States, Rex Donald.

"Ah, Mr. President, good morning. How's the weather in Washington?" I tried to muster a buoyant response, but I really intensely disliked our newly installed president. However, I figured it was best to feign friendliness and rise to the occasion, especially given that he had already paid me millions and much more was to come.

"Don't waste my time, you little asshole. You know why I'm calling."

"The subject is deceased. I finalized our plans last night. It's over."

It was surprisingly easy to lie.

"Far fucking out," replied the president, always vulgar. "At last, now I can get on with our real business."

I think I now knew whom he meant by "our." My dreams had informed me. I had just told President Rex Donald that I had delivered a gift to him of such great import that even that narcissistic clown could not contain his glee.

"Yes, sir," I replied.

"We've got some financial business to discuss. Come to the residence. We'll tie up loose ends. Get here."

Click. He was gone. No goodbye, just an abruptly terminated telephone call. Rex Donald was a beauty!

OK, I was sent to handle Dr. Marshall. Fortunately, nature took care of that for me, but I saw no reason not to claim credit.

A quick jump in the shower, then rigorously toweling off, a quick call to my pilots to let them know I was on my way, and back to the chifferobe to dress.

My clothes were gone. Gone! Instead, a black leather suit and crimson tunic hung over calf-high boots. These were the clothes in my dreams.

That son of bitch: Merlin, Dr. Marshall. What doors to the universe had he opened, nonpareil dimensions I had never witnessed? This was magic, but it was not black magic; it smelled of jasmine and sage, it was safe, it was kind, it was heavenly.

I understood now the meaning of Dr. Marshall's note and my dreams. He had laid this all out for my perusal and my unconscious review. And he had done it from the grave.

I screamed with amazement, delight, a sense of being overwhelmed, and stupefaction, recognizing that I had crossed over into places imagined but rarely, if ever, seen. I started to laugh — at first just a chuckle that quickly erupted into a feeling of euphoria I had never before known. I fell to the floor, spread eagled, now in apoplectic delight.

The laughter turned to tears, pouring and streaming down my cheeks. My body shaking, clattering out of control; I was gasping for breath, feeling skipped heartbeats. The enormity of this supernatural experience completely humbled me. Blessed but humbled.

How had this happened? Perhaps, as my dreams had instructed me, it was *my* time in karmic space, a culmination of eons of existence resulting in these dumbfounding dimensions: Why fight a wave so great?

It took some time for me to regain enough composure to pull myself together. I knew that Dr. Marshall had invested me with a mission, which I wholly embraced even knowing that carrying out his instructions could result in the end of my life.

I had never been ready to die. For all the killing I had done in my life, death was the only thing I really feared. Now I knew there was a reason to give my life: for the sake of all.

Maybe this was the reason that men in war have stormed beaches facing certain death, numb to their dismembered comrades scattered, in bloodied parts, before their feet. Was I now seeing the same sense of right these millions, through the ages, had seen? Was this the transcendental ladder that made the giving of one's own precious life worth sacrificing?

The flight back to Andrews in Washington was like a flight to my ultimate freedom. I was emboldened. Soaring over the country had always left me with an exhilarated feeling, flying above the clouds, musing about how such distances had been laboriously crossed by the country's earliest settlers, about how our native tribes survived for thousands of years on this amazing and diverse land.

Except for the Air Force steward and pilots ensconced behind the locked cabin door, in the high-flying plane, I was very much alone.

Or so I thought.

As I turned my gaze from the oval window back into the cabin, there — quietly, saffron colored robes spread in perfect array, shaven head radiant and glowing in a golden hued appearance — sat Dr. James Marshall.

Yep, dead or alive?

I had long since passed the point of surprise.

"Dr. Marshall, I thought you were... gone."

"Santiago, I thought I told you not to be concerned with trivialities. The distance between earthly and eternal living is a matter of perception, not reality. The universe does not destroy the souls to which it has given rise; it repurposes them."

"Dr. Marshall, far be it from me to take issue with you!" I laughed. He had already blown my mind. I knew I was safe in his presence and that forces far beyond my perceptions had carried us both on some ecstatic wave.

During my dreams, I had never once touched Dr. Marshall. Now, for no particular reason, I reached out to put my hand on his knee. I felt a need to *feel* him; I don't know why. My hand fell through air: there was only the appearance of a knee, a convincing appearance but nothing physical, just light, pure light. Dr. Marshall was there, yet he was not. We both understood.

"Santiago" — he spoke without the use of audible words — "We can forego the mechanics of moving lips and tongues; they just slow things down, don't you think?"

Another one of his surprises: telekinetic communication. OK, why not?

"Santiago," he continued soundlessly, "I've come to discuss your impending meeting with Rex Donald, our illustrious president. I've thought quite a bit about whether some ultimate demonstration of compassion is in order, if there was even a glimmer of hope that it would make a difference. But Rex is a molecular moron. There is not one atom in him which is not wicked, ignorant, devilish."

"Your letter made that abundantly clear," I said out loud, because that's just the way I do things. "I am ready to do as you ask. Nothing would give me greater happiness."

"Good. Now, for the mechanics." Dr. Marshall reached over and placed a small titanium vial in my hand.

"Poison, Dr. Marshall?"

"The most potent nerve agent in the known universe. We had it synthesized at our Sandia Labs at Kirtland Air Force Base in Albuquerque. It's really quite special, typed for your DNA and his. Alone it is innocuous, but once you touch him the compound will become fully activated. *Finito! Hasta la vista. Comprende, ¿amigo?*"

Telepathic Castalian: There's a rare skill! What genius! More miracles from Dr. Marshall. Expected.

"The potion will put you both to sleep, as if dead. It affects the DNA, and even to a skilled pathologist it will appear the end for both of you has arrived. But you will both recover, several hours later, probably chilling in a Washington morgue. You will go on to happier days and he — well, let's just say I have a suitable surprise for El Rex." Dr. Marshall pointed to the vial: "We call this concoction the Lazarus Liquid. Cute, don't you think?"

"Cute" was not exactly the word I would have chosen, but I had become used to Dr. Marshall's quips. So much so that I could no longer distinguish the actual from the fantasy — or was it the other way around? I have to think about this; unwinding sorcery is not a game for sissies.

Brilliant doctor. We both smiled.

"No sense wasting an enlightened being — too rare a breed, especially these days!" He grinned.

"OK, Dr. Marshall, what have you planned for Oedipus Tyrannus? Death? Slow death?"

"You know, Santiago, I have been mulling this over now for quite some time. Death for this miscreant would bring me pleasure. But it's actually a kindness I have no intention of extending to him. He always wanted to get his hands on, well, *everything.* So, an appropriate, ultimate punishment suitable for his crimes and sordid intentions needs to involve him getting his hands on *nothing.*"

"What do you mean, Doctor?"

"You'll see, Santiago. What I can tell you is that revenge is a dish best served cold."

Odd, this all: having a telepathic discussion with a hologram. Not just another day at the office!

21

Deep State

As we soared along, Dr. Marshall continued our holographic dialog.

"Santiago, I want you to understand in a bit more detail about what has been called the *social contract*. Among the several reasons that I consider creatures like Rex Donald to be such bad actors is not just that they overtly lie and connive. Make no mistake: their lies are not trivial. They are deliberately intended to deceive, to sway opinion, to promise without intention of fulfillment. Our public has suffered, and the distance between the elite and the rest of the population is immeasurable. The financial establishment has been consolidated, and is in the hands of a very few. Minds are controlled by dulling the reason of the people and keeping them stoned on a supply of dope provided compliments of groups like the CIA. Crimes like this are blamed on cartels and drug lords, when in reality the government is the pusher. Their reason for being is self-preservation, which means taking out as much as possible and putting back little or nothing.

"Who makes up for the shortfall? A shortfall where the few, the ultra-rich, corner all the wealth and control. They can afford to game the system with shell corporations, tax shelters, harboring money off shore, laundering funds, bribery at home and abroad: the list is endless and out of the grasp of most. These kinds of moves are completely out of the reach of a *wage earner* who is holding on for dear life.

"While the responsibility of the elite hides in the shadows, the burden of making war, building roads and schools, and oversight over the integrity of the environment and the food supply falls, more and more, on those who struggle daily with simply staying alive, one paycheck away from oblivion.

"After World War Two and the boom of the 1950s — when I was a kid — moms could stay at home while dads went to work. There were *families*. Now, nearly every household requires that *both* parents work. Kids are shuttled off to day care or grandparents, or left to their own devices.

"The tax rates which fall on people who often are confronted with having to choose between food and medicine are the highest in the world. What they get in return is decreasing dramatically. The message is clear and simple: suffer and pay. This is slavery. Poverty is the most vicious form of repression. Why would those in power make that wish? I firmly believe that poverty is a weapon. Placing people on the edge introduces a convenient distraction: those struggling to survive are unlikely to revolt!

"People stressed by decreasing access to medical care are worried about their own survival. They have neither the time nor the energy to worry about the well-being of society.

"What better way to control vast numbers of people than to keep them under the thumb of the government, to invade their privacy, and to shift the burden of taxes and debt service onto those who can least afford it? This is not social policy: it is tyranny.

"It is no accident. It is not an oversight. It is contrived and deliberate. The Deep State is a different beast from the State intended by the Constitution and the laws of the land. The Deep State has sordid intentions, first among them being domination.

"Desperate people, people desperate to hold on, are an easy target for propaganda. We know this; it is not a secret. We hear about how major corporations control the government, but fail to really understand how this filters down onto the front porches of the average citizen.

"The strategy is to blame others. Anyone. Distraction works. The diversion of attention results in obedience and compliance. Compliance is good; resistance is bad.

"They sell snake oil: better health care for the public while concurrently slashing funds to maintain a well population. Who would believe these lies? Pissing on the shoes of the people while telling them that it's raining. Who would believe such trash? Yet this is the bill of goods sold daily to those who are ignorant and desperate to believe that they are getting a straight deal. And they buy it, perhaps out of desperation, ignorance, or stupidity, because keeping the public stupid enables control and domination.

"It's not just that Rex Donald has access to nuclear and biological devices, to massive military organizations. That would and should be enough. No, Santiago, it goes much deeper. These lies are real expressions of condescension, contempt, and disdain.

"Yet, the lies are bought wholesale! Will this grass roots support erode before the final nails are hammered into our social coffin? I'm here to shine bright lights, in hope that the perversion which has befallen our culture is arrested once and for all.

"The social contract is an old understanding. People invest the government with power in exchange for protection of their well-being. No amount of lying and disingenuous crap can ever ultimately hide treachery.

"Rex Donald may try to run a deep state, but he cannot stand up to bright lights shining. Anton Molinov need make no pretenses: he already has constructed a government where torture and suppression are understood and universally feared. One can get away with murder if people are cowering in terror.

"The Mob, *à la* Gentile, makes no bones or formal pretense. For him, it's about pure power and money. Those who get in the way, die!

"This is not a broken social contract, it's a complete negation of it. This is what we now collectively face. This, distilled, is the confrontation between good and evil, between dark and light."

22

The Reunited Nations

"SANTIAGO," CONTINUED DR. Marshall, "We have an awesome responsibility to shoulder. I have set out to change the complexion of the world order. You know what has been done to bring us to this moment: the lives given, the fortunes spent, the millions upon millions whose lives depend on what happens next.

"All of this has been foretold in your dreams. I think you got the point!

"In 1947, after World War Two, when the United Nations was formed, and shortly after I was born, the world had just begun to emerge from an epic horror. So much needed to be done. Many were resolute that the insanity of war should not be repeated. So, first in Lake Success — on Long Island in New York — and then in San Francisco, great people convened with the intention of forming a world-facing oversight body, a kind of global government. The United Nations.

"The Rockefellers, who owned a tract of land the East Side of New York City, around 44th Street, donated a strip of land to the governments of the world. It is now the home of the United Nations. A wonderful complex sitting on the East River in New York. That building was a symbol of hope. It still is, but the United Nations has been on a very rough ride. From its beginning, even though the idea of world oversight was and is noble, the private and separate agendas of many have pulled and tugged, resisting the idea of a coordinated planet.

"The United Nations has been starved for money and resources by those most able to afford it — most ignobly by the United States. I have previously explained to you that the United States, although a symbolic participant, has really had no intention of being subjected to the oversight of anyone. So, through death of a thousand cuts, the hope of a united world has turned into a hobbled illusion.

"I do not discount much of the great work of the UN, but the great powers want to remain great and separate. There is symbolic participation, but the heart of the world does not beat at that great edifice in New York City. I wish it did.

"Along with the emasculation of the concept of international citizenry, real corruption has occurred: theft of money, obfuscation, and debasement of purpose has seized many parts of the global operations of the UN. What a shame — a tragedy, really.

"As we stand at the edge of real change, the UN needs to be reconsidered. I have set in motion a purging of the bad apples. Their punishment needs to be public and definitive. Those responsible for the perversion of the great intentions envisaged in 1947-1948 need to be isolated and completely shunned.

"I have called for a conclave of the world's great minds to reimagine the United Nations as the Reunited Nations. As soon as Rex Donald and Anton Molinov have been appropriately neutered, the process of reinventing a world-facing oversight body will begin in earnest. I and my friends and colleagues from around the world have dedicated our fortunes to make this wish a reality.

"A lot has happened since the founding of the United Nations. The world has become a deadlier place. The chance of a fatal mistake has never been higher, and the polarity of thought around the planet is unprecedented and pulled taught, ripping us apart and bringing our species to the ultimate brink.

"The selfish, like Donald and Molinov, who are neither American or Russian, cannot be tolerated. Their kind cannot, and should not, rise up again. They desire control over every living soul. This must not be."

Dr. Marshall was, in every way, a world citizen: a man with a soul and a heart beating with compassion for us all.

23

The Residence

THE TOUCHDOWN AT Joint Base Andrews was uneventful. Our shining white Gulfstream taxied to a small, nondescript Quonset hut at the far end of the field. A black, unmarked Ford and liveried driver met me as I descended from the deployed ramp of the aircraft. Without a word, the driver took my small crimson leather satchel, and we were off.

The drive to the White House is about twenty miles. It was about 6:30 a.m. when we passed through the gates and guardhouse. In the light of early dawn, gardeners were already clipping here and there; as usual, the grounds were groomed like one of Donald's golf greens. He liked his grass to be perfect!

After passing through security at the South Portico and walking through the Diplomatic Reception Room, from the Center Hall I rode the elevator to the second floor. When the door opened, I was greeted by an usher, who steered me toward the East Sitting Room.

Suddenly President Donald appeared at the end of the hallway, clad only in blue and white striped pajamas. He hated the White House. For his luxurious tastes, he had once explained, it was far too primitive. I reminded him that it was good enough for Kennedy, Lincoln, and the dozens of others who had come before.

His unhesitating response: They were pigs.

Standing there in his pajamas, he glared at me. "What the fuck are you doing dressed like a Slovakian motorcycle cop?"

I had forgotten that I was now wearing my Marshall uniform of black leather and crimson.

"Oh, I decided to change my look, Mr. President." I was deferential; after all, the man owed me and I didn't want to jeopardize payment.

"You look fucking ridiculous!" The president had a limited vocabulary, mostly consisting of profanities and monosyllabic thugster jargon. How did he ever rise to this level of power? Probably lawyers and political handlers! I wouldn't trade places with them for all the tea in China! Like trying to teach a snake to speak French. Can you picture the abuse they suffered with his filthy mouth and his foul being?

"Let's go in there." He pointed to the door of the Lincoln Sitting Room.

"Sir, may I please use the W.C.? It's been a long trip."

"All right, but make it quick. I've got a lot on my mind. Today is going to be highly unusual."

Unusual indeed: Dr. Marshall had painted the picture clearly. Today, President Rex Donald was to make his move by suspending the Constitution and instituting martial law.

It had to be today!

The timing of my dream, the arrival, the command to return to Washington from Santa Fe — all were no accident. The pieces were coming together.

"Yes sir," I said. As you walk down the short hallway into the Lincoln Sitting Room, on the left is a private restroom — the Lincoln Bath. I went inside, shutting and locking the door behind me. After quickly accomplishing my real-life biological business and washing my hands, from my pocket I removed the small titanium vial Dr. Marshall had given me. Nothing holographic about it. I carefully removed the rubber stopper as Dr. Marshall had instructed, and placed a small drop of its clear fluid in the palm of my right hand. It quickly disappeared into my skin — seemingly intelligent, strange. This concoction had been compounded for my DNA and Rex Donald's.

The game was in motion!

Stepping back into the hallway, I entered the Lincoln Sitting Room to see President Donald sitting in a high-back armchair upholstered in green leather. After pointing to the door and making a gesture for me to close it, he motioned to me to sit down. I did.

"So, he's dead," said the president. "You're sure?"

"Yes sir — he's fucking history." When in Rome, speak as the Romans do. "I loaded him the trunk of my car and dumped his ass in the middle of absolutely nowhere. By now, vultures should be enjoying his carcass for breakfast."

As I lied, it gave me pleasure to play with the president's toy brain. He always cooed when people spoke to him in the only language he understood: crude and rude.

"Good, very good!" He smacked his hand on his knee. "I always hated that prick. We've had our eyes on him for a long time. We know about his control centers, armies, associates around the world, the counter measures he was planning. We've just been waiting for him to make a move. He always wanted me gone. He's the one man who always concerned me. The rest of my enemies were easily neutralized. Not Marshall — too smart, too rich!

"So, Santiago, we made a bargain: Twenty million dollars." From the breast pocket of his pajama top he took a slip of paper, which he thrust at me. "Here's the wire transfer confirmation to your Panamanian account. It will be deposited in two hours, when their banks open for business."

I didn't touch the paper. "Sir, I was expecting cash. That's what we had agreed to."

"You don't trust the president of the United States? Santiago, you little shit!"

The truth is that I didn't and never had. How could anyone in the right mind trust a man like Rex Donald, known for being disingenuous, not to mention disgustingly self-aggrandizing, with pictures of himself hung in gold frames around the room? The man was in love with himself — and himself alone.

"Take it!" he thundered.

I had no choice. I took the paper and without looking at it slipped it into my pocket.

"We're done," he said. "Leave, and while you're at it, get rid of those ridiculous clothes. They make you stand out. Around here, no one stands out but Rex Donald."

"No problem sir." With a smile, I reached to shake his hand — the touch for which Dr. Marshall had so painstakingly planned.

President Donald did not shake my hand. Instead, with a smile he looked at something over my shoulder. I turned around in my chair. Two armed guards, very large men, dressed from head to toe in Kevlar, carrying automatic weapons, had silently entered the room and now stood behind me.

"You really think I was going to pay you, you stupid moron?" sneered President Donald. "Leave you to tell the tale? You're have always been a pawn — one of many on my payroll. So, Santiago, you're fucking *fired*!" He burst out laughing. It was strange because I had never heard him laugh before.

The guards stepped towards me. In one continuous unconsciously choreographed sweep, with my open hand I reached out to Rex Donald, president of the United States, and gave him a hard slap across his cheek.

24

No Exit

I AWOKE. STRETCHED OUT on a slab. I knew not where. The place was dimly lighted. The stainless steel table beneath my naked body, cold. Not pleasant.

From somewhere in the room, I heard the sound of a radio or television. "The president of the United States was assassinated this morning at 7:15 a.m. Washington time,' said the voice. "The vice president, Admiral Arnold Schwartzer, will be sworn into office as the next president. Chief Justice Harding is now on his way to the White House to perform the ceremony. God Bless America."

The White House press secretary had, in his breast pocket, quite a different announcement: the announcement of Donald's imposition of martial law. That would have to wait. Shit happens!

What President Rex Donald did not know was that the military was set to foil his plans: They would not enforce the martial law he intended. Marshall had conferred with them all, in the U.S. and around the world. Without their power, he was impotent. As for the planned financial takeover of the world's money markets, Dr. Marshall had also seen to it that countermeasures were in place to take effect concurrent with the declaration of martial law. Domestic and international money transfers, SWIFT, would be highjacked, castrated, halted. No power, no money — no nothing!

Lying on the carpet in the Lincoln Sitting Room, President Rex Arnold's seemingly lifeless body had been examined by the physician to the president and photographs taken before being ceremoniously lifted onto a stretcher for removal to Walter Reed Medical Center for the autopsy.

In the Queen's Bedroom across the hall, the vice president, Admiral Arnold Schwartzer, had been bedding Donald's wife. They had been awakened by the commotion following the apparently fatal slap I had planted, lovingly, on the cheek of the inert president.

Schwartzer was a puppet and a lackey. You may ask, who of any substance would stand behind a scum like Rex Donald?

Someone who wanted the special perks of the job.

Mariana Alexandra, Mrs. Rex Donald, had been fucking the vice president for several months. Mariana was a Romanian prize wife, several decades Rex's junior. The president knew all about it; in fact, he liked to watch them frolic between the sheets — a specially installed one-way mirror in the Queen's Sitting Room provided him a bird's eye view of their lascivious amour. I am told that Rex enjoyed pleasuring himself, concerned only with his self-serving passion and stoked by theirs.

Mariana was in the marriage not for love but for the money and prestige. I am told that she had confided with her close friend, Contessa Romano, she had closed her eyes wide shut when she and Rex Donald had consummated their marriage, resulting in their only child, whom they called Duke. Duke! Why not King or Emperor?

Back to the morgue. My morgue. I had the vague sensation of being lifted by attendants and placed into a box. The lid was closed, then to a waiting hearse and a short ride to a cemetery, probably somewhere in the hills of Virginia, far enough distant from Washington, with no one around to observe.

I was now fully conscious: being caged in a coffin was hardly enjoyable and getting a little stuffy. I felt the box being set on the ground and the lid opened.

Standing over me, smiling, was Dr. James Marshall.

"So Santiago, you were supposed to shake his hand! My men —Donald's guards — told me it didn't go as planned. I should have predicted that he would try to screw you. Twenty million dollars was not the point; revenge and your silence were his true intentions. Rex has always been transparent, too obvious. Will wonders never cease?"

"How are you, Dr. Marshall?" I asked as I sat up in the open coffin, my back and knees stiff.

"Free from having a body is really quite remarkable!" he replied. "I have always sought the light; now I am the light!"

"Yes sir, I can appreciate that."

The attendants helped me out of the box. I stood on the bare earth. I was naked, and they handed me my clothes — my now-familiar leathers and crimson.

Ah, so much better!

"So, Santiago, care to accompany me to New York City? Ever been to the updated World Trade Center? Quite magnificent — I think you might like the view."

"Lead, sir, I'll follow." I had to remind myself, time and again, that Dr. Marshall was only known to me in my dreams and as a spirit. I had grown fond of him as a concept of a man; not a man of flesh, rather a man of mind and light. The illusion of his existence was profoundly convincing, but only a wholly believable figment of my perception. Ah, Dr. Marshall, you devil!

"Two scorpions in a jar!" Marshall quipped.

"What the hell does that mean?"

"The Secret Service guys transporting his body to Walter Reed are part of our team. They will take him to a different destination. There will be a decoy body, some poor indigent camped in Lafayette Square, opposite the White House. Poor bloke had overdosed during the night, as many do. Utter poverty a stone's throw from the center of global power and wealth: unflawed irony! I wonder how long it took the Army pathologist to figure the ploy?"

Dr. Marshall had, as I had come to appreciate, an irrepressible and very twisted but wonderful wittiness. Fun with holography! I must be mad, but after a ride on Dr. Marshall's merry go round, who cared?

"Santiago, I had mentioned to you that I had been cogitating over an appropriate fate for Donald and Molinov. You know they deserve each other: birds of a feather. Are you familiar with the writings of the great French philosopher and existentialist, Jean Paul Sartre?'

"Yes, of course I know the name but I'm not terribly well read, and am not genuinely familiar with what he wrote or thought."

"You're forgiven, Santiago. One of Sartre's great plays is *No Exit*. One of my favorites. *Huis Clos*, in French. The play teaches that hell is other people, locked together, forever, without chance of escape. Time is suspended, bodily needs — food, water, sleep, and biological necessities — no longer exist. That sort of thing. It's staged in a chilled room with no doors, no windows, nothing — just others, closed together, naked, for the rest of time.

"Given the intentions and the horrendous crimes contemplated by Rex Donald and Anton Molinov, killing them would not provide the kind of punishment suitable to their terrible offenses, real or intended. No, something more choice, that's the thing. It finally came to me. Doom them to hell, forever, together.

"I was set to include Gentile for a stay in this eternal hotel room, but his lovely bride handled that for us. Unfortunate — he was spared the never-ending pleasure I had planned for them all."

Riding the Amtrak train, we pulled into New York. At Pennsylvania Station was a waiting limo. As we walked side by side through the terminal, Dr. Marshall was visible only to me. I was sure I did not talk to Dr. Marshall during our stroll from trackside to the curb of our waiting stretch.

You can get arrested for hallucinating in New York! Commuters, beware!

We arrived downtown at One World Trade Center. The highest building in the Western Hemisphere, it's exactly 1,776 feet tall, a number deliberately chosen for its significance. Security had been prearranged as we boarded the elevator to the top.

As the elevator door opened, the presumed dead president of the United States and his Russian counterpart, Anton Molinov, stood before us.

"Ah, my dear Rex. Hello Anton, long time!" exclaimed Dr. Marshall.

"Marshall," spat Rex Donald, "you fucking piece of shit, don't you know who your messing with?"

"Yes, Rex, as a matter of fact, I know exactly who! Has no one informed you that you have been declared dead? You once wielded great power, and now you are powerless."

"Dr. Marshall," President Molinov said, "You know you'll never get away with this. My agents will track you to the ends of the world."

Dr. Marshall burst into laughter. "The world is it, Anton. That's the problem about being so self-engaged. Same for you too, Rex. Your greed has blinded you. This world, which you have both sought to buy, is but a speck in the cosmos. You stupid little boys are prisoners of your own limited minds. I would help you, but I know you both too well. You both were born under bad signs — *hopeless* signs.

"You did hear about Gentile? He realized we were closing in on him, and escaped to Palermo for a facial, so to speak. Read, identity change. Thanks to his lovely wife, he will *not* be joining you both for your extended vacation in hell."

"What are you talking about, Marshall?" said Rex Donald. "What are those ridiculous robes you're wearing? What's with your shaved head? Have you lost your fucking mind?"

"Quite the contrary, Rex: I have finally managed to find it!"

"Marshall, you piece of dirt, you have stepped over the line." Rex was defiant. "I am the president of the United States! You are and always have been irrelevant!"

"Irrelevant?" said Dr. Marshall. "Interesting choice of words. But then you have always been educationally challenged. I'm delighted that your elevated station in life has opened your eyes to new words in our language.

"I seem to recall that your talents as a kid were limited to frying ants with a magnifying glass as they were fleeing back to their ant holes in the sidewalk cracks — remember? I also recall that the infliction of their death provided you with remarkable delight. That's when I realized that something deep inside of you was, to put it gently, warped, perverse.

"You do recall, of course, our discussions about nuclear weapons. You thought they were a great idea. You didn't understand why they weren't used more often. Rex, you would have dropped one on the anthills of our youth. Thank God your daddy didn't give you a few for your amusement.

"The problem, my dear Rex, is that you *did* have these weapons, tens of thousands of them. As a kid you were only a play-acting fool, but now that you have grown, you are a real fool, and quite a dangerous clown. You never had any regard for human life as a kid; it was limited and relegated to the limitations of your fantasies. You have had every intention of realizing your fantasies! I cannot, I *will not* allow that."

Marshall was closing in on Rex Donald.

"You would kill millions to distract the eyes of the world from who you truly are. You would impoverish the world to suit your purposes. I know you. *I know you!*"

"What are you talking about?" sneered Rex Donald.

"Come, come Rex, let's not play, shall we? You don't remember our discussions about nukes as kids? Well, I do. As a matter of fact, I have tapes of our conversations. Meaningless, really, until you became president. Those childish tapes carry an historic imprimatur. They reveal your real mind. What's always been in your thoughts: wanton destruction."

"You little fuck," said Rex Donald. "When we were kids you recorded our conversations without asking me? Without me knowing? Why did you find them so noteworthy?"

"Rex, that's a very good question. I guess even as a six-year-old kid I had some glimmer of understanding that you, supported by your father, might ultimately ascend to something more than being a spoiled, out-of-control brat. It was just an intuition, a child's look into the future. Right on target, I would say!

"Now, I think that, as history records your legacy, those recordings will help inform posterity of who you actually are and always have been." It seemed that Dr. Marshall was prescient and had finally arrived at the ground zero target he had seen so many years before.

"No one will believe you!" insisted Rex Donald.

"We'll let history decide that, Rex. I also have copies of your books."

"What books are you talking about? I never wrote any books, you scumbag!"

"Oh, Rex, Rex, you were a prolific author: have you forgotten? Your books — your *financial* books. Your creative accounting logs: one for you, the other for the government and your duped partners. I never understood why such fraud coursed so freely through your veins. Tax fraud, money laundering, mob deals, wire fraud, kickbacks: do we need to go on with the sordid details? You wrote the book. No need to preach to the choir!"

Dr. Marshall was at it again: he loved his quips. I grinned.

"Rex, *amigo,* I have them all!" continued Dr. Marshall. "I think the public you have so skillfully deceived will find that their hero ain't no hero. I intend to enlighten the millions you have fooled along the way that their emperor is as naked a jaybird."

"How did you get them?"

"Ah, Rex, you underestimate me; probably always have. When you embarked on your real estate escapades, I planted people in your offices. My people, not yours!"

"You did *what?*"

"Come, Rex, we're both adults. You were always a criminal: first as a child, and now, far worse, as a man, at least until I put my foot in the door. You can't help yourself. Your felonious instincts are part of your biology. They are you, you are them.

"You probably won't be happy to know that *all* of these will soon be published world-wide. I have also built a research library, in your memory. It will contain your entire archives. Researchers, for centuries to come, will be able to feast on the wretched trail you have traveled, now fully exposed. The world needs to know the crud whom the American people, stupidly, elected as their leader. My hope is that exposing you and your family will shut the door on anyone even closely resembling your rise to the presidency and the power you have grabbed."

"Marshall — Jimmy — let's work this out," said Rex Donald smoothly, like the con artist he was. "I'm sure there is some way for us to clear the air."

"Rex," replied Dr. Marshall, "You are completely predictable, like a crooked slot machine at one of your failed casinos. Not even with fixed tables and a three-million-dollar bailout from daddy were you able to make enough, so you stuck it to your partners and the banks. They must love your ass!

"No Rex, you see, there is nothing you have I need or want. I have amassed a great fortune — a *real* fortune. You are nothing more than a debtor to the world. Buy me! You're a dreamer!"

"Wait, I'll give you anything you want," said Rex Donald, his doughy face now showing an expression of desperation. "I'll repent. Yes, that's it, I'll repent. That's what you want isn't it? For me to say I'm sorry?"

"Rex, if I asked you to repent, really repent, you'd want to know what I meant! That's exactly the problem: the tip of the spear. You don't have the slightest idea. To repent, you'd first have to ask me what I meant. That's the heart of the problem and reason that we are today gathered here, standing at the edge of forever, your eternity.

"No, Rex, I'm going to provide you and your buddy here, Anton, ample time to figure out that there is no repenting for the fundamental evil which you both embody. Perhaps a few hundred million years will do it. These years will be measured in seconds, and every one of those moments will slowly tick, like chilled molasses. You might eventually open a window into something you have never known: compassion, real compassion, not merely the pretense of compassion, of repentance. I'll know when and if that moment ever arrives."

"How will you know?" Donald demanded.

Dr. Marshall smiled. "As I said, Rex, you have no idea who I am. No, Rex, no more paper roses. It's over! I'm cashing in a lifetime of your stolen chips."

Anton Molinov said nothing. He was a bare-knuckled Russian. He knew the brutality of truth. No fancy dancing your way out. Why bother? I think that all Anton craved was another shot of vodka, perhaps a double. Unlike Rex

Donald, he understood Dr. Marshall. Where Rex had spent his life dreaming of dominance and destruction, Anton had been fully engaged. He was a killer from the day he was born. Rex was a bush league player who had ascended to true power, while Anton always possessed the power and brutality to which Rex had only aspired.

"Now what?" Rex realized that he had been painted into the ultimate corner.

"Rex, you know so little about me: who I am, what I've become, where I'm going."

"Where are we?" Rex demanded.

"My dear Rex, we're where you always wanted to be: where everyone can see you! Regrettably, you will not be able to see them."

"What the fuck do you mean?"

"Time enough for that, time enough." Marshall motioned to me. "You know Santiago, no?"

"Of course," replied Rex Donald. "He's my guy, or at least I *thought* he was my guy. He's a hired CIA operative turned murderer for hire."

"Yes, that's who he was, but he saw something you never did, perhaps never will: light. Santiago has become my student. I think he's ready for graduation."

Exploding with emotion, Rex Donald suddenly made a wild swing, aiming for Dr. Marshall's face. He wound up a punch and leaped forward, hoping to destroy Dr. Marshall, screaming at the top of his voice as he did: YAAAAAAAAAAAAAAH! As his closed fist swept through the air, it passed through the likeness of Dr. James Marshall — the daydream of Dr. James Marshall.

Nothing. A swing through thin air.

"What the fuck is going on here, Jimmy?" Rex Donald, the supposedly dead president of the United States, was stunned, perhaps for the first time in his life. Stupefied, disbelieving what just happened. He reached out to touch Dr. Marshall. Again, nothing. Zilch.

We all stood in the presence of the supernatural: a state of authenticity where fantasy is real and the tangible is illusion. It was too much for Rex Donald. Anton Molinov already understood that he had fallen helpless to his fate.

Rex Donald staggered back. The reality or lack of it had completely blunted his senses. Every instinct, every sense he had ever known or felt had evaporated. He dropped to his knees, staring at his childhood friend, Jimmy Marshall. Rex Donald began to cry and weep.

Molinov was too hardened to emote. He had spent most of his life in a deep alcoholic stupor; he had hallucinated the dead rising and walking. For him, the scene was just another segment in the deluded movie of his life, beginning on the frozen plains of the Siberian tundra.

For Rex Donald, this was something new and unbelievable. He had spent his silver-spoon life believing he had control of everything. Now he was frozen, mortified, paralyzed by the realization that he had dominion over nothing, not even over his own senses. People are restrained in padded rooms for less. Rex would soon find out that his new forever home was worse, much worse.

"Santiago, do you recall our discussions about the difference between wrath and anger?" said Dr. Marshall, coolly, as if Rex Donald's violent outburst had never happened.

"Yes, sir."

"I have given myself to the pursuit of compassion, not punishment. Yet, ironically, we stand here on the verge of inflicting an ultimate punishment. It gives me no pleasure. I don't hate Rex or Anton. I am reviled by what they represent, not who they are. They are simply messengers of the darkest forces lurking in the corners of the cosmos. They have been mere carriers of that gloomy message and acquired the means to inflict horrific harm and suffering on others. Left unchecked, their intentions would have become manifest. You know that I could not, would not, permit that."

Dr. Marshall placed his spectral hands on the heads of Rex Donald and Anton Molinov, who were now both bowed in submission before him, on their knees. These great thugs, on their knees, brought finally to heel.

"Now for some magic, Santiago," said Dr. Marshall. "I hope you don't see this as a theatrical trick. It's a necessary component of my plans for these boys."

Dr. Marshall uttered several phrases in a language I had never heard. He removed his hands. "Touch them, Santiago."

I placed my hands atop of each their heads. My touch met with no resistance. Like Dr. Marshall, they were there, yet they were not.

"Stand up, gentlemen," said Dr. Marshall. "I have relieved you of the burden of biology. You now exist only in thought. You will never hunger again, never sleep again, never hunger for anything. Your lives will go on unburdened by the earthly wants or requirements. You are now pure spirit: dark spirit, but nonetheless spirit. The only physical sensation you will experience is cold: frozen and thawed then frozen again, in an endless cycle. You will also spend eternity in complete darkness. This is a special hell reserved for those whose karma has earned them a status far below that of even a cockroach. Don't blame me: You bought this ticket."

"Why?" Rex whispered, "Why?"

Ignoring his entreaty, Dr. Marshall said, "Allow me to show you to your new quarters. Santiago, better that you stay here. I'll return shortly."

Rex Donald and Anton Molinov had become completely obedient. They stood, and Dr. Marshall put his hands on their shoulders. With Dr. Marshall between the two of them, they walked straight ahead and disappeared through the solid wall atop the tallest building in the most vibrant city of this world.

A few seconds later, Dr. Marshall emerged from that same wall. He looked at me, squarely, eye to eye. He radiated a golden light. His skin was unblemished, perfect, and his saffron robes, flawless, with his crimson sash tied impeccably around his waist.

I heard a whooshing sound.

"What's that?" I asked.

"Hot lead being poured into the hollowed cement blocks which make up the walls to the eternal chamber which now entomb Rex and Anton. It will block any electromagnetic radiation, like radio or internet waves. *No Exit* — it's done!"

"What's in there, sir?"

"The cold end of time."

25

On The Edge

"SANTIAGO, NOW WE must look ahead to what's next."

"Dr. Marshall, I'm overwhelmed."

"I understand, I understand. Staring down evil, calling it for what it is, putting it down, wrenches the gut and disrupts the soul. You have reason to be incredulous.

"Let's take a ride, Santiago. Have you been to the United Nations recently?"

During the ride up the FDR Highway to the exit at 44th Street, Dr. Marshall and I sat side by side: me in body, he in spirit. As we rode, Dr. Marshall placed his hand on my left knee. I experienced a surreal flash of energy through my body. Marshall had never touched me before.

"I told you it was graduation day for you, Santiago. Congratulations: you can now live in body and spirit forever, should you wish. Your mission, should you decide to accept it, will require continuity spanning many lifetimes. You will need to oversee the slow transition of the global unconscious from accepting and respecting greed to fully rejecting it. Let us not fool ourselves: We cannot simply wave a wand and instantly expect that human beings will be able to see evil and dark when, we as a species, have been blind to these sinister forces that exist in others.

"We have been taught in so many ways, in every way, that words don't mean what they mean. We are taught to disbelieve our senses and our instincts. Language is manipulated, ambiguous words are chosen to cloak the real intention of the speaker. Leaders say, "We favor a diplomatic solution" for this or that, while guns are locked and loaded. We are told that we live in a great democracy while blatant dictatorial edicts strip rights and render Constitutional protections void. The sad, the amazing part of this, Santiago, is that it is so widely believed! Believed!

"Had we not disposed of Rex Donald, he would have tightened the noose and moved to assert purely tyrannical powers. Who is to say that his successors will not do the same? The stage has been set for a step change on a domestic and global basis. Rex Donald, Anton Molinov, and Luigi Gentile are symptomatic — they *represent* the problem, but they are not the problem itself.

"I don't know whether the generation of politically correct millennials has unwittingly paved the way for totalitarianism in our time. What I can tell you, as a product of the 1960s, is that we were on the streets. We stormed the cities, we descended on Washington, we shamed and pushed Nixon out of power, we stopped the Democratic political machine in Chicago, we made our voices unmistakably clear that the Vietnam conflict was wrong, we lambasted President Johnson who, despite his muscular political agenda, left Washington rather than seeking another term as president.

"Do you see that kind of fervor now? No. You see obvious abuse inflicted by large corporations on a confused and dazed public willing to be kicked, time and again, in the shins, waiting for days in emergency rooms for care rendered by progressively more poorly trained doctors and a medical system which has become an industrial machine rather than a system to deliver care and succor. The insurance industry has consolidated into a Mafia-led cartel reaping profits while denying benefits, a few remaining banks collectively holding a pistol to the head of the world economy demanding subsidies to make up for their thievery, threatening that there will be a global collapse if the people don't pay up!

"Banks have consolidated, with the big eating the small. They wield enormous power over the government. You will recall that in 2008 they staged an attack on the public by claiming that unless they received massive bailouts, the world economy would fall into shambles. That was a lie, which triggered the injection of one hundred billion dollars a month into each of the ruling monopolistic banks. Most of that "bailout" never trickled down to the public. Rather, the pockets of the bank executives were generously lined, leaving the public to pick up the debt the government sustained to keep them afloat. It was a scam.

"There are now only a few major media companies. Whether they can be accurately accused of mind control is debatable, but certainly possible. As good journalism has died due to severe cutbacks within once-respectable news organizations, there are fewer well-trained reporters keeping track of the shenanigans of the kleptocracy: this is no accident.

"Ultra-conservative groups have made massive investments establishing departments and chairs in major universities to assure that the minds of the young are amply dosed with right wing propaganda. They have taken a long view and it has been working. Even our greatest academic institutions have suffered from the injection of insidious mind control — a devilish and deliberate business.

"The societal body politic has become infected and malignant. The scene has become insane! Yet every day a large portion of the populace swallows these bitter pills and pays the inflated bills.

"What kind of a mind would accept this mutant strain of abuse? I will tell you, Santiago: a mind that has been invaded, deliberately perverted, and manipulated by its masters.

"The two criminals we have just dispatched are merely messengers. We need to be focused on the message! Their individual personalities are really distractions designed to divert attention from the poisoned rivers that flow deeply into our lives and minds.

"Generations will need to be purged and re-educated. Illiteracy, which is now prevalent, is a vicious manifestation of suppression. The power of the written word has been neutered. The populace relies not on education, reflection, and thoughtful examination but what they see on screens and what they are told by talking heads. Again, no accident.

"Ignorance opens the door to mind control. Poverty seals the deal."

Dr. Marshall had again hit his stride. His footsteps of thought left a thunderous vibration, reverberating with undeniable truth. I felt humbled in the presence of this phenomenal master.

We arrived at the United Nations, where two new towers were near completion, standing tall on either side of the iconic thirty-nine-story building.

I turned to Dr. Marshall. "I was unaware that new towers were being built here on 44th Street. Do you know what this is about?"

"Santiago, the United Nations needs to Re United! This requires that diplomats from around the world be educated by the finest minds in the world. I have arranged a United Nations University to be established with the express purpose of educating world leaders and their representatives. These buildings are two of several; other such universities are being constructed in Geneva and in Beijing.

"The people of the world must come to know one another. It's harder to hate someone up close. Developing a universal zeitgeist requires education, both intellectual and spiritual.

I am certainly not suggesting that inherent, embedded cultural differences will exist. I have no intention of having people abandon their national identities. I do, however, believe that a world consciousness needs to be developed and fostered through personal relationships and education. The leaders of tomorrow must learn very new skills and they need to know that we are all floating in the same boat.

"As for the issue of education: One illiterate person, anywhere, is one too many! Think of it as arms forged into intellectual plowshares. This is, of course, a massive undertaking. The task will take, by my estimate, at least one hundred years. I want *you* to supervise this mission, personally, as my emissary."

"Dr. Marshall, this is a bit over my head — beyond my pay grade, so to speak."

"Don't worry, I will guide your hand." Dr. Marshall gushed with a joy I had not seen him express. He had seen the future — a future of hope.

"Profound economic changes must also take place," he continued. "The world is running out of natural resources. We can barely sustain the seven billion people living on the planet, and conditions promise to get worse, with pressure on water, air, food, and medical care. We are brothers and sisters, whirling in space, locked in an awesome embrace.

"The change of history will require people with magnificent, inspired vision, understanding, and pure compassion to affect these planet-saving changes. They are mandatory and unavoidable.

This will not be easy. Failure to break the march of humankind towards self-immolation must cease, forever.

"The miracle of life is a gift we must preserve. Light must overwhelm dark. You and I were born, Santiago, forever entrusted with this stunning responsibility.

The dark days of the oligarchs, the thugs, are over. Tyrants must never be permitted to rule again. They must be permanently exiled and torn from the pages of history. We must *act* as one species because we *are* one.

"Santiago, I urge you to accept our awesome covenant. You will rise to the occasion. I will be by your side until the end of time."